A
Childhood

A Jesus Childhood

Carl W. McClure

iUniverse, Inc.
Bloomington

A Jesus Childhood

iUniverse books may be ordered through booksellers or by contacting:

iUniverse
1663 Liberty Drive
Bloomington, IN 47403
www.iuniverse.com
1-800-Authors (1-800-288-4677)

ISBN: 978-1-4759-4082-4 (sc)
ISBN: 978-1-4759-4086-2 (hc)
ISBN: 978-1-4759-4083-1 (ebk)

Library of Congress Control Number: 2012913778

Printed in the United States of America

iUniverse rev. date: 08/09/2012

CONTENTS

Acknowledgments

I want to thank many people who gave me ideas and encouragement while writing this book. This book has been many years in the making. Writing it has been an on-and-off process, but mostly "off," put up on a shelf for months on end with no thought of the next sentence. Finally sometime in early 2009 I decided that I would either finish it or forget it.

The first thanks goes to my brother Dale who suggested I write a short story about the life of Jesus. We were standing in his living room. I remember my response. "Everything to be written about Jesus has been written already. What is left that I can add?"

He said, "You'll think of something."

His words stayed in my head and I began to formulate an idea. What about a story of his childhood before age twelve? That seemed to be fertile ground for new fiction.

Along the way and especially early in the process, Kathy Lee prodded me on and kept giving me new ideas to try. I was able to write most of your ideas into the story; a few didn't fit. Thank you, Kathy, for your suggestions.

Many thanks go to Margaret Estes who dug into my manuscript with gusto and covered the pages with editorial comments after I thought it was "done." You were merciless in your editing and for that I thank you.

My brother Earl gave me many comments to incorporate, and I did. He was able to think like he was living back in that era, and that added to the authenticity of the storyline. Thanks, Earl.

Dale's wife Judy and her friend Sharon Miller gave me an earful when they set me straight on several points of accuracy in the Bible. I incorporated most of your suggestions that made the storyline easier to understand. Thanks to both of you.

Thank you to Reverend Donna Johnson, former senior minister at Unity of Fairfax, Fairfax, Virginia, for your kind remarks and thoughtful suggestions. You do not know how many times I scribbled notes from your message onto the weekly bulletin for use in this book.

Thank you to Reverend Sandra Butler of Unity of Fairfax, Fairfax, Virginia, for your inspiring messages and evening classes that gave many ideas for this book. Your encouragement kept me writing.

Thank you to Reverend E. J. Niles who is on staff at the Unity Institute and Seminary, Unity Village, Missouri. You encouraged me to research this subject meticulously. Thanks for helping me write a good book.

Thank you to friends and neighbors Harold and Barbara Goldman for reading an early manuscript and for your helpful insights into the Jewish culture. Thanks, Harold, for the prayer in Hebrew.

Thank you to June Wagner for gifting me your personal copy of *Metaphysical Bible Dictionary*, which I used in depth. It made my job easier. Thank you, June.

Thanks and blessings to my patient and loving wife Nancy. You encouraged me to write and edit, especially near the end; you kept me on track. Plenty of times you knew when I needed quiet time. After I thought it was "done" again, you read it aloud to me. Wow, what a difference your suggestions made to the overall feel and flow of the storyline. Thanks, Nan.

Thank you to God for my daily inspiration and for showing me when to write and when to quit. Like any artist, I was never quite satisfied. There was always another idea to add or a paragraph to move. It was hard to put the pen down for the last time.

Introduction

You are reading an account of Jesus that takes place from before his birth through his twelfth year. The storyline is not typical of what we know about his life. Several scenes in the book deviate greatly from tradition. Perhaps the most obvious deviation is the time between Jesus' birth and his family's return to Nazareth. This book portrays a longer stay in Bethlehem than what Matthew and Luke suggest, and that deviation introduces a chain of other events that are new to this book. The list of discrepancies between this book and your conceptions of Jesus' biography may be a long one.

Throughout the story, I have incorporated references to *The Twelve Powers of Man*, as introduced by Charles Fillmore, who with his wife Myrtle, began the Unity movement quite unintentionally in 1889. It was continual prayer, they believed, that healed Myrtle's chronic tuberculosis and Charles' leg injured in childhood. Their healing encouraged them to establish prayer circles in private homes in the Kansas City, Missouri area where they lived. Those prayer circles later became known as Silent Unity, now a twenty-four-hour prayer service. The Unity School of Christianity evolved, as did a robust publishing business from the printing of a newsletter that circulated to all of the prayer circles. Charles Fillmore became a devoted student of philosophy and religion, and wrote extensively on those topics.

The Unity movement is a worldwide Christian organization that emphasizes a positive approach to everyday living. It teaches that God is the one power, everywhere present, divine energy. Each of us is an individual expression of the creative God, the good; therefore, each of us is inherently good. Jesus, our Way Shower, is a master teacher of universal truths. I have illustrated my understanding of those concepts throughout the book with dialogue and description.

First published in 1930 by Charles Fillmore, *The Twelve Powers of Man* is a treatise on discovering and activating the twelve spiritual abilities, or powers, that each person possesses. Each power has a definite body location, color, and purpose. As a teaching tool, many organizations assign a power to each month of the year. Additionally, each power is assigned to one of the twelve apostles. Of course, the apostles and later the disciples did not exist at the time this story takes place. Jesus expressed perfectly each of these spiritual powers through his day-to-day teachings. Look for a **bold word** followed by a discussion or a dialogue that illustrates each power as depicted in the story.

To best understand how you can relate to each power, I suggest that after you read how the power influences the story, pause to reflect on its meaning. Reread the passage, perhaps aloud, and think how that situation or those words can give meaning to your personal life. Maybe a brief meditation would help you to become perceptive to the divine activity taking place within you. Balancing these gifts with daily experience will lead you to inner peace and perfect harmony. Remember, you possess within your consciousness these twelve wonderful gifts from God.

The powers appear in *A Jesus Childhood* in this order: Release, brown; Power, purple; Will, silver; Understanding, gold; Faith, dark blue; Order, dark green; Love, pink; Life, red; Wisdom, yellow; Imagination, light blue; Strength, light green; and Enthusiasm, orange.

When you see *words in italics*, know that they are thoughts of characters. One character's thoughts are particularly astute; his name is Ilan and he does not speak aloud.

At times, the characters speak words and think thoughts that are not consistent with their way of life. They receive their inspiration as a gift from God who speaks to them softly. Often in our daily lives, we say something and do not know from where it springs. We are acting as a hollow reed that allows words from some unknown, higher authority to simply flow through us. That is exactly what these characters do. They are divinely inspired in word, thought, and deed.

The Bible is a finite document. By that I mean there are a limited number of inspired writings that are included in it. Historians and archeologists have uncovered much material written around that timeframe that is not included in the Bible. Some of that missing material does not agree with the writings in the Bible. People of the time did not know or care to record every meeting, every event, or every conversation that occurred. Most of the traditional stories were recorded years or even decades after the fact, being based on word-of-mouth, handed-down legends. It was my honor as an author to invent scenes and dialogues that help to illustrate what may have occurred at the time. Many references I consulted offered confusing and often contradictory information.

For example, one source said Mary was thirteen at her betrothal, while another source said she was fifteen. One book said that all citizens had to travel to the house of their origins for the census, while another said that only the men had to travel, and could represent those in their families. One reference said that the City of David was Bethlehem, while others said the City of David was Jerusalem. Sources conflict as to when Jerusalem was the capital of Judea. One source said Jesus was born at an undated midnight in December of 4 BCE. Another source said that Jesus was born on August 21, 7 BCE; this is the date I selected for this story. It falls in the Jewish month of Elul. That means in this story, for example, when Jesus is four years old, the year is 3 BCE. There is no year "zero."

Here is another contradiction. Tradition says Jesus was born in a manger. Some sources say he was born in the home of a member of Joseph's extended family who happened to live in Bethlehem. He may have been born days after they arrived in the city. Maybe they moved to the grotto after his birth to accommodate the large number of curious people who wanted to visit the newly expanded family.

After studying several biblical references, as listed in the bibliography, I learned that many figurative passages found throughout the Hebrew Scriptures were subsequently misapplied to the life mission of Jesus. Scribes often distorted many Scripture passages in order to make a given episode of the Master's earth life fulfill the prophets in the Scriptures. The early followers of Jesus often succumbed to the temptation to make all the olden prophetic statements appear to find fulfillment in the life of their Master, no matter what he did or said.

I wrote the story from the viewpoint of that time era. That is, I used words or phrases that ordinary people may have used. For example, I used the word "adz" in place of "axe." I used the word "yestereve" in place of "last night." A beautiful aspect of any language is that it evolves according to the new generations of people who use it. Language is not static, but rather it is dynamic and flows sometimes like a trickling stream and at times like a rushing river. The same applies to traditions, customs, and ceremonies; they change.

As another example of evolving language, I wrote that Mary and Joseph's betrothal was an exceptionally binding agreement, far more of a binding nature than our current day usage of the word "engagement." The betrothal was the main event; the marriage ceremony was less important. After the betrothal ceremony and before the wedding, each partner lived in their childhood home with their parents for one year and they were forbidden to engage in marital relations. In modern times, the Jewish betrothal ceremony and the wedding ceremony have become blended into one ritual.

In *A Jesus Childhood*, Mary and Joseph do marry, although I do not describe it. I reference it only in a thought-conversation when Mary and Joseph prepare to flee to Egypt with the infant. The betrothal takes place in the summer of 8 BCE. Their flight to Egypt takes place in 6 BCE.

The Talmud, in its many variations, did not exist as we know it during the lifetime of Jesus. I struggled with presenting facts in the Talmud without its having been written down. All I could do was to refer to it as being incomplete and in a state of continual evolution. The Jews believe it was revealed to Moses along with the Torah. The Torah is the first five books of the Hebrew Bible. The Torah was allowed to be written down when Moses received it, whereas the Talmud was handed down orally. The Talmud was finally chronicled between the second and fifth centuries with commentary by the most prominent of rabbis of the time, adding further minutiae to the already jumbled, incoherent, and incomplete legends. The finished work is large like the ocean and choppy like the waves.

Translating one language into another is a complicated venture, especially if the alphabet is different for each language. Hebrew is a stylized variation of the ancient Aramaic. When Hebrew is translated into English, the spelling of a sound becomes difficult because different translators spell the sound differently. For example, the Hebrew word for the betrothal ceremony is Kidushin. It could be spelled Quiddushin and still be a valid word in English. Sometimes the English version of a word contains an apostrophe and sometimes it does not. For example, the Hebrew word for wedding is Nisun or Nissu'in. It is the sound of the word that is important.

In Jesus' time, the writings known as the Scriptures constituted their Bible. Today we call those same Scriptures the Old Testament. The New Testament did not exist in Jesus' time. The religion called Christianity did not exist in Jesus' time. The concept of Christ was not yet conceptualized. Chapter divisions and verse numbers were not part of the original manuscripts. The geopolitical area known as Palestine did not acquire that name until the first century CE; it evolved from a Roman designation of that region they called Palaistine.

Mary may or may not have been a true virgin in the sense that we use the word today. During her lifetime, the term "virgin" meant that she was a young woman, and nothing more. The term "priest" in this story refers to any man who was in a position of spiritual or religious leadership.

The number of male infants under two years of age living in Bethlehem at that time could not have been more than two dozen, based on the then-population of five-hundred to eight-hundred. The killing of those children in an obscure Judean community would hardly have attracted the attention of the scholars in that part of the world. That episode was merely another of Herod's many rants against his Jewish subjects. My description of that event is disturbing.

Every story of Jesus' life is a bit different from the next, and this one is likewise different from any you have read before. By no means is this story meant to be the authoritative source on Jesus' early life or to take the place of the established, more scholarly texts on the subject.

When you, the reader, are inspired to read this book, may you simply place yourself in the mindset of living two thousand years ago in a faraway country. That means, for instance, thinking like a Jew in Jerusalem or a Roman soldier occupying that land. Reading historical fiction gives you the chance to go places you have not been and to experience, for example, the many odors drifting from a synagogue, the sound of a Passover feast, and the sight of a camel caravan crossing the desert. Use this book as your passport to go back in time to visit a foreign land.

CHAPTER 1

Spring 8 BCE

〜〜〜

Visions

My heart shakes like a tambourine at Passover! And I know why.
It is because of him—him!—that man, up there, standing under that
old olive tree. He is at harmony, yet the mob of people around him is
boisterous. The hubbub! The din! The clatter! I tremble from the noise,
but more from the peace I receive from his words.

Crowds flock all around him. His face is calm; he wears a modest
woolen garment. He enthralls. He teaches. He preaches. The people flock
from villages near and far. All are here. I see rich. I see poor. The lame
and the lepers are here, as are the farmers and shepherds. Women and
children are here, too. People yearn to hear what he says. They reach out
to him. I see one woman fall to her knees, crying tears of joy, and throw
her arms open to the sensation around him. They touch his garment.
They kiss his sandals. They do anything to feel oneness with him.

"Quiet! I must hear this man speak!" shouts a man.

"His words! Listen to his words!" A woman is desperate to hear his
discourse.

He does not raise his voice, yet all can hear his message as clear as a
cymbal. His face radiates love. The man's words mesmerize me, for they
are as a riddle. My heart pounds inside my chest as I repeat his words in
my mind trying to understand his wisdom.

Ach! What is this? Now I see a tiny baby, an infant. This baby boy—how beautiful he is! He is pure and innocent. And his aura; how it glows! The baby is wrapped tight in clean swaddles with a man's mantle rolled under his head. He lies in a bed of fresh hay on a crude wooden feeding trough. The baby sleeps with a gentle smile on his face. I can see he is content. Near him I see his mother, a radiant young woman. There is a man, too, the baby's father. They seem to be settled in a sort of grotto, in a place I do not know. What am I to learn from this?

I hear a voice whisper in my ear—no, cry into my head! "The child—you must protect the child! It is imperative to do so! He is as innocent as the stars are unnumbered!" I quake in my sandals. The voice continues. "The child will grow into a man of great consequence. His teachings will live on forever. He is long-awaited by your people. It is your duty to help him grow into manhood. You are to teach him, to guide him, and keep him safe from harm. Be his friend, give him love, and provide him guidance. This is to be your life's work. Abide these commands greatly."

Now another crowd engulfs me all around. I am consumed with the mixed passion of it all. This multitude is even more frenzied than the first one. I stand in the middle of these mad people. They jostle and tumble all about in turmoil. I hear shouts and screams. None of the faces do I recognize; none of the people do I know. Lights flash in the sky. Thunder beats upon my ears. I am disoriented on this hillside. Roman soldiers are here in great authority, and in great numbers. The soldiers are intent on the execution of a man—do I know him? Women and men are crying and wringing their hands in anguish over what they see. One woman falls to her knees, wailing hysterically, shrieking and pulling at her hair in frustration. She loves the man passionately. It takes four soldiers to pull her away from the crude cross. She does not notice the blood dripping onto her scarves.

The mob screams over the din, "Stop the foolishness. This man is innocent and without blame. He has done nothing wrong!" A shiver races up my spine. "The man is not guilty of any crime!"

The man hanging there is stripped nearly naked of his clothing. His hair is unkempt. Red trickles from his side. I cannot stare at him for a long time, but only take quick glances. The images I see imprint on my brain. The man's death is imminent. I would pray for his soul, only my heavy breathing and racing thoughts take priority. Somehow I force a supplication for him.

Suddenly, like an earthquake, the violence on this hill shakes me awake. Sweat drips from my face. I cannot breathe; I cannot move from my pallet. I rub the sleep from my eyes. Was I dreaming? What is the message? What am I to do?

Chaim

"He is my friend and I love him." I cannot stop saying those words. Everyone calls him Jesus except his mother. She calls him—ach! That is for later.

I want to tell everything I remember about his life, as best I can, as much as I can. I do not know why or how, but I am compelled to relate this narrative. I make a vow to myself to do so. My memory is not sharp like an adz any more, and I cannot write in words. Neither can I read those words that others have written. I have never attended school. By a miracle that I do not understand, I am able to recall those events around the boy Jesus. I am not a scholar.

My name is Chaim. It is a strong name and it means in Hebrew, "Life." My intuition allows me to see the events and hear the words around him, even though I am absent from him. Compared to my friend Joseph, I am an old man because I have seen the tunnel of time pass before my eyes more so than he has. That gives me more than five decades of wisdom. For my age, I am strong, and I am strong because of my work. I think of myself as not handsome. I am an ordinary man living an ordinary life. My strongest desire is to relate this story.

I am not a married man any more. My wife Chesed, which means, "Mercy," died last year of a terrible disease for which I have no name. She gave me three decades of dedicated marriage. In the end, her body withered in size; she stopped eating and felt pain throughout herself. She slept to flee the pain. She said there was a hard swelling, like a stone, deep inside a secret part of her body that she would not disclose to me. She told me that the swelling was the source of her illness. She simply became quiet, save for her painful outcries, and wasted away. The physician could not heal her. In the end, she became incoherent and spoke in tongues. She passed peacefully in my arms. She left me with two daughters; both of them are married in the village.

Release. Losing my partner was hard. Words do no justice to the intensity of my feelings. As many times as I have cried in my sleep, she will not be here in her physical body any more. It is because of this knowledge that I release her now. I let her go fully and without condition. The brownness of my life I accept. I pray to God to give me color in my eyes, to see the world as beautiful once more.

I let go of all that stands in the way of God's good for me. I let go of all negative thoughts, feelings, and beliefs from my consciousness in order that new thoughts may come to me. I have no fear, misunderstandings, or sorrows. All is good and all is perfect. I forgive and I free my mind and body from this loss. I am transformed by the renewing of my mind.

Mary's House

I build houses. My sweat exchanges for my wages. The houses I build are practical with a beauty of their own. Within my group, I am the one to mix the straw-and-mud mortar for those who affix the stones together.

Each house attaches itself to the next one to give strength. Many times the houses arrange around a central shared courtyard and well. The women take turns carrying water from the public well to their homes. Everything looks like the earth, for everything is from the earth. Earth represents those material thoughts that are part of each one of us. Any contrasting color comes only from the garments the people wear and from the earthenware they make and decorate. The women adorn their homes with flowers and plants, and those colors make me happy.

Most houses I build are small and have but two rooms. As an example, I describe the house where my friend Mary lives with her parents. I am familiar with it; I helped to build it. It is located not far from the central part of the village.

The entrance is a plain, open doorway covered with a drape. Pulling the drape aside is the way to enter the house. The front room holds the meager furniture, consisting of a low table made of cypress as the main piece. Surrounding that are three stools and a lampstand that bears the single oil lamp. Mary's loom and yarns fill a corner. In another corner are an arrangement of stone dishes and stone pots and a small collection of earthenware eating utensils. Rolled up are the woven sleeping mats made of reeds. A small mat covers the stone and earthen floor.

The room in the back encloses the oven and the mill for grinding grain. Mary operates the mill alone, but it is easier if one of her family helps her. One person turns the grinding wheel and another feeds the grain into the slot that funnels the grain to the wheel.

Nearby this back room is the animals' annex. In this simple shelter Mary keeps the family's donkey, a goat, and a few chickens. It serves as a storage place for the extra clay jugs and a few sheepskin rugs. The sides are wood and mud up to eyelevel, where they become open to the weather. Rough-hewn logs hold up the roof.

Mary's Wish

I overheard Mary talking aloud one day in the oven room. Her parents were not present, but the donkey was standing in the stall nearby. "I wish I had someone to help me when I grind the grain for my family." She sighed in mild frustration as she poured the barley down the slot. "Maybe I could hire a young boy from the village. He would make my grain grinding easier, and I would have more time to weave scarves on my loom."

Mary knew the value of keeping the donkey. She stroked him tenderly, and talked to him as if he could understand her every word. Some days she thought she heard him speak, and she carried on a full conversation with him. When she went about her daily duties, he watched her, for he had nothing else to do except swat the flies with his tail. When sleepy, he locked his knees and slept standing up. He knew his place in the family and he was obedient and faithful. Indeed, he was highly respected in every way because he gave Mary freedom to travel about Nazareth and the countryside.

I am here only to be truly helpful.

A Growing Friendship

What a fine woman Mary is! I know her character. She maintains high standards for her appearance and for the appearance of her home. She dresses modestly, keeping her head covered properly.

I am honored to know Mary. Her twinkling brown eyes reflect her character, purity, and grace. Ever she is cheerful and bright in her disposition. She expresses her feelings with respect. She wears a faded cerulean mantle, as that is her favorite from her youth, and a matching tunic. She is an exemplary neighbor and I think she will be a fine mother when the time comes. Her face emits a radiant countenance. She is intuitive and wise; she knows the Jewish laws and can discuss them in detail. Being a woman bars her from doing so in public, but I know that she would if she were permitted. In private with our mutual friend Joseph, she expresses her viewpoint vigorously on many subjects.

Everyone knows Mary. Everyone admires the works she performs. It is not beneath her to wash the clothes of the elderly or to mend the rips in their mantles. She sweeps the public courtyards and carries water and charcoal for the lame. In her spare time, she delivers honey cakes and lentil soup to the elderly. From her mother, she learned the household arts well.

One of Mary's pleasures is gardening. Of all the gardens in her neighborhood, her family's is the most prolific. It is behind her row of houses and she can walk to it in two minutes. Early one morning, I was walking where the gardens grow. Mary was there already, busy tending to each plant as required.

"*Boker tov*, good morning, Chaim. I am pleased to see you today."

"Good morning to you, Mary. How is your garden this fine day?"

"It grows well. Can you see the new growth coming in? Look over here. See? This row is cabbage, this one is leeks." She smiles with pride and shakes the dirt from her hands. "Here are turnips and lettuce."

"Is that the row of lentils?" I point.

"It is, and over there are the beans and peas. I am pleased with God's handiwork."

Mary feels fulfilled when her garden includes watermelon and cucumber. Near the front entrance to the garden, she cultivates a small plot of herbs—mustard, chicory, and cumin. And not far away she nurtures a small grove of mulberry trees. From the mulberries she ferments a small quantity of sweet wine for her family and neighbors.

Another way Mary keeps busy is nurturing a friendship with our friend Joseph. Joseph and Mary have known each other from the time of their childhoods, since they live only a few lanes from each other in the village. Even their parents are friends with each other.

I am proud to know Joseph. His visage is strong for a young man. His beard is growing in full and square, and his hair grooms near to his shoulders. When I look into his eyes, they sparkle with the joy of youth.

His wardrobe is customary and proper, being woven of simple brown broadcloth. Underneath is his tunic. Over his tunic he wears a mantle. Wrapped tight around his waist is a leather sash. On hot days, he wears a headband around his forehead to keep the sun and perspiration from his eyes. He owns one pair of sandals, as do I. Joseph keeps his head covered properly at all times when in public. He knows the laws well and abides by them faithfully.

He is mild in manner but strong in character. He is conscientious with his duties, and faithful to the religious practices and conventions of our people. He speaks calmly, and says only what needs to be said. The plight of our people causes him much sadness. He hopes one day to become a prosperous and independent builder in his own right. Ach! Joseph is a blessing in my life!

CHAPTER 2

Summer 8 BCE

Joseph's Regret

As the relationship between Mary and Joseph evolved from friendship to love, I knew that this was an important time for them. I saw that Joseph was nervous as I helped him carry a large lumber to his workshop.

"Joseph," I asked him, "What is wrong?"

"It is my age. I am eighteen years now. I have been very busy with my carpentry business. And because of my dedication to my business, I placed my friend Mary in jeopardy."

I asked, "In what way?"

"I delayed my social responsibility toward her. Do you know she is fifteen years of age already? She is nearly past her decisive years of marrying." He looked distressed. "I have delayed her marriage too long."

He took a deep breath and studied my face. "Chaim, she is almost past her prime years; she is nearly a spinster! She is two years beyond the age when all of her friends became betrothed. Most of the women here in Nazareth are married before age fourteen, you know that. What have I done to her? She did no action to deserve this tardiness in her life. I deprived her of her full womanhood by delaying our betrothal and wedding ceremonies. It is because of my self-centered interests. I feel responsible for her disappointment."

He looked at me intently. "I want to marry her."

"Calm yourself, friend, for you have done no wrong. Your dedication to your livelihood is your only misjudgment, and that is certainly no cause for concern. Be peaceful on yourself."

Negotiations

A few days passed. The first step Joseph took to fulfill his wish was to tell his parents of his interest in Mary. Of course they knew that! How could they not? He told them because our tradition is for the man to tell his parents. Then they deliberated his request at length. They emoted greatly and wrung their hands in anguish. They spoke in loud voices and paced the floor. They satisfied themselves that their son was genuine in his request. In time, when they had satisfied themselves of Joseph's sincerity and love for Mary, they paid a formal visit to Mary's parents.

It is our tradition that the parents of the groom-to-be visit the parents of the bride-to-be and ask that the two children be allowed to betroth and marry. The groom-to-be is not permitted to ask the woman directly for her hand, nor is it permissible for his family to ask the woman for her hand. Both families deliberated. Full negotiations ensued.

Today is the day that Joseph's parents arrived at Mary's parent's home, and after the full and formal greetings concluded, including serving fresh water to drink, the negotiations began. There was nothing to hide. All the neighbors knew what was taking place behind the draped door; it was the planning of a strategy to unite their children. By tradition, Mary did not know of the deliberations. By realistic fact, she knew all. Like all women of her age at this important stage of her life, she had dreamed and imagined of this event for many years.

Joseph, still somewhat naïve in this matter, thought the whole issue still unresolved. He did not know why his fellow tradesmen, myself included among them, made him the butt of gentle jokes. We stroked our beards and smiled inside.

The formal discussions went on for days; it was part of the ritual to do so. Mary's family had no dowry, as her economic status was the same as Joseph's. Neither family made any concessions because the groom-to-be was in good health and was able to care properly for his wife.

One obligation of these negotiations was the part where Mary's parents invited Joseph into their home to question him on his knowledge of the Tanakh. The Tanakh is a collection of knowledge based on the

Torah and the Talmud. The higher Joseph's score, the more worthy he stood in the eyes of Mary's family.

The word Torah means, "Teaching" or "Law." The Torah comprises the first five books of our Jewish heritage, and those books are Genesis, Exodus, Leviticus, Numbers, and Deuteronomy. We Jews read it and know it as a great mosaic of information.

The Talmud comprises a large collection of traditional Jewish knowledge, and it is entirely unwritten. God handed it down to Moses with the Torah.

To no one's surprise, Joseph answered every question fully and with much fluency.

Ah! At last I saw the families emerge from the home. The two mothers and the two fathers agreed; the Kidushin would take place in the month of Tishri, late this summer. The Kidushin is the betrothal ceremony, and carries the weight and solemnity of marriage itself. This formal betrothal holds the highest esteem in Jewish law. Even though the wedding had not occurred, Joseph could not be released of his obligation except through formal divorce. I know Joseph; that would not happen. After the Kidushin, both of my friends continued to live as before, Joseph in his home with his family and Mary in her home with her family.

To show the solemnity of the Kidushin, if Joseph were to die between that ceremony and the marriage, Mary would become his legal widow. According to custom, the pair will spend this waiting time for the Nissu'in—the wedding—in searching for a small home and furniture.

The Betrothal Ceremony

Kidushin began with Mary's friends gathering at her house to wash her and dress her.

"Mary, we are here to help you prepare for the biggest day of your life." Speaking for the women was Hadas, and her name means in Hebrew, "Myrtle Tree." "We, all of us here, have been friends since girlhood and we want this day to be most meaningful and most memorable for you. We love you and give you blessings on this day. Your mother is here with us and she is most proud of you this day."

Mary blushed as her friends washed her face and arms with warm water scented with lavender. They were sure to place seven petals of myrtle in the basin as a symbol of love and good health.

"We selected this raiment for you to wear. It is the freshest and newest of all we have in our possession, and we know it will serve you well. Here, let us help you into it. You are beautiful."

Next they anointed her skin with olive oil and cinnamon. They spared no expense in making Mary ready for this day. "Now we scent your clothing with myrrh. It is to remind you of the beauty of God's abundant garden."

"I am blessed."

Hadas continued with the preparation. "Now is the time that we suspend a sachet of powdered myrrh lightly between your breasts. Myrrh, as you know, has many forms and uses, and this day we use it to make you ready to receive Joseph's love even more fully. *Ihulim levaviim.* Best wishes unto you."

The bride-to-be blushed softly. She was ready. This preparation was a ritual Mary had dreamed of since she was a little girl.

I saw Mary now as she came out of her house. How excited she was! She strode on the streets in the main part of our village with an air of pride; soon she would be Joseph's intended! From the courtyards and the few balconies, people threw roasted wheat at her. On the cobbles in front of the pageant, children spilled wine and oil and strew what few flowers they plucked. People danced in the streets, played flutes, and beat tambourines. All the while, Joseph led his own procession on nearby streets, and soon mingled with Mary's parade to form a grand procession. From all sides the couple heard joyous singing.

The ceremony was formal. They entered the groom's house, or more specifically, his parents' house where he still lived. Their friends led first Joseph and then Mary to the canopy called the chuppah. That is because, by tradition, the man of the house must be there to welcome the bride home and because, according to the Scriptures, man was created before woman. Under the chuppah, Mary circled around Joseph seven times to signify a seven-fold bond that was to develop between the bride and the groom and their families. Joshua circled the wall of Jericho seven times and the walls fell down. So, too, after Mary walked around Joseph seven times, the walls between them fell down and their souls united. Seven is the number most often found in the Scriptures.

What followed next was important. The rabbi read aloud the ketubah, or betrothal contract. The rabbi then read seven blessings, after which the bride and groom drank wine from a common cup.

11

I saw this clearly! Joseph stepped on the cup to shatter it, symbolizing the cup to be the oneness of the couple. I heard it shatter. Our tradition dictates that when the cup is shattered, the couple enters a state of devoted attachment from which they will never emerge. The rabbi read selections from the ancient scrolls and said a blessing for the newly joined pair. Then they entered the seclusion room, away from the guests, for a reasonable time together, after which they reemerged to greet and congratulate their guests and to celebrate. Now they were truly betrothed.

The Feast

I was nearly exhausted because of all the excitement, but I could not cease my account. Daylight faded and evening fast approached. The feast was perfect. I saw neighbors and friends bring foods, each as each could. Lamps appeared to illumine the evening. Garlands and greenery adorned the walls. From nowhere materialized salted fish, pickled fish, baked and broiled fish, and minced fish. Fish arrived that was boiled in milk and fried in egg. Mints flavored the muttons perfectly. Served, too, were cheeses, watermelons, leeks, onions, pomegranates, sweet breads, and almonds. One neighbor brought sweet dried figs and a paste of delicious salty olives in oil. Is not God good to us to provide such abundance?

I know Mary. I know she understands the true meaning of the feast. The true meaning is that which results from the union of man with the Spirit of God. When this union takes place, man eats of the heavenly manna and drinks of the living waters. It is opening the divine potential to each man and woman.

Chapter 3

Summary 8 BCE

Zacharias' Prayer

At the same time that Mary's parents and Joseph's parents were negotiating the details of the betrothal, an auspicious event occurred in the Temple in Jerusalem. Zacharias, the husband of Mary's cousin Elizabeth and priest in the Temple, had been offering prayers for Elizabeth to bear a son. Because both Zacharias and Elizabeth were quite old in age, they had long ago given up hope of conceiving a child of their own. It was their age and dedication to the laws that made them most respected in their community.

It was while Zacharias was blessing incense in the Temple that an angel of the Lord appeared to him. The angel stood at the right hand of the altar—the most holy of places—where Zacharias was blessing incense. Zacharias became frightened and did not know what was happening to him, as he had not seen an angel in all of his long years of life. He composed himself while the angel prayed for him.

"Do not fear, Zacharias," the angel said reassuringly. "Your prayer has been answered. Your wife Elizabeth is ripe and will bear you a son. You will name the boy John. He will be the cause of much joy and will be great in the sight of the Lord. He will be filled with the Holy Spirit even from his mother's womb. He will grow up to guide many souls to God; he will gladden many hearts. He will turn the hearts of countless people in Israel to the Lord their one and only God. He will proclaim the coming of the Heart-Healer of your people."

Zacharias quivered as a branch on an olive tree in a zephyr. "Angel, you are the first I have seen in my long life. I trust what you say to be true. I bless you for your prophecy. You know I love my wife and I want only good things for her. I, an old man, say unto you that my wife is advanced in her years and no more is youthful. Are you sure she will be able to bear our son without any difficulty of childbirth? How will she cope with her old age and become young as a new mother again? I do not doubt the uprightness of my wife, but I do question her gift of maternity."

The angel was patient. "Fear not, Zacharias, fear not. Your wife will be strong. She will be youthful again for this important task. Your son will grow and mature to become a leader of men of your tribe. He will emulate the spirit of Elijah the prophet and cause many people to ponder their lives and change their unholy ways. He will lead many people to seek God. He will prepare the common masses for the coming of the real Lord, who is still in heaven."

"Bless you, angel of heaven. You impress me greatly. Tell me more, but do not tarry with your words." Zacharias wanted to know more about the angel's message, but being the diligent worker of God that he was, he was growing impatient with the angel's persistence.

"The infant will flourish in the Temple," the angel continued. "It will be your responsibility to teach him the ways of the Temple. You will be the one to illustrate to him the implications and understanding of the laws. He will present to you and your wife the needs of any typical boy."

Zacharias was mounting disbelief with the angel's persistence, for he needed to return to his duties in the Temple and continue blessing the incense for the crowds waiting outside the gates. "Who are you? Tell me, what is your name so that I may be satisfied that I am not seeing an impossible vision?"

"I am the angel Gabriel who stands before the one and powerful God. I am here to speak to you, old man, to announce to you the good news of your wife. However, because you did not believe my words, and because of your impatience in hearing God's word in your ears, you will become speechless and unable to have full mind until all of these things take place. You will be as an empty wine skin because you will have no words to flow forth from your mouth." Being finished with his mission, the angel whispered a secretive prayer over Zacharias' head and vanished into a wisp of a cloud in the heavens.

The crowd outside the Temple had become restless, as the time Zacharias had consumed was far beyond what was normal for the blessing of the incense. When he finally appeared at the archway to the courtyard, the men saw that he was unable to speak. They realized that he had seen a vision. They knew this because Zacharias could only gesture but not speak. He continued for some days to complete his duty silently inside the Temple, and then traveled home to a small village named Ain-Karem to be with his wife.

The angel Gabriel had prophesied correctly. Elizabeth was indeed ripe with child. She went into seclusion to thank God for his mercy toward her. "The Lord has finally blessed me and taken away my disgrace before others. I can now be as a real woman and bear a son for my husband."

Upon his return to his pastoral duties in the Temple, Zacharias brought Elizabeth to the altar and allowed her to speak on his behalf. She announced the name of the boy to the throng. "His name will be John. His name will be John because that is a strong name and my husband, as do I, feels obliged to let this strong boy grow up with a strong name to match his temperament."

The crowd gasped. "No, it cannot be! Why? What do you mean? What are you doing to this infant? Who is John? There is no one by that name in this family!"

The men roused Zacharias to the center of the court. "Zacharias, we know you cannot speak, but, *bevakasha*, tell us please, what name do you give to the baby?"

Taking a writing tablet, Zacharias wrote carefully and slowly, "His name is John."

Everyone was shocked. At that moment, Zacharias' voice returned and he began to speak, clearly and loudly, as if he had not been mute at all. Assuming his authority from his years in serving the Temple he began to thank God for all of the wonderful things that had happened. "Thank you, Spirit, for all of the good things you have given to Elizabeth and my family and to me. My heart is glad and my tongue rejoices for my son John and for the good health of my dearest wife Elizabeth.

Thank you, Blessed Spirit, for all things spread before us on this table of life."

The priest Zacharias was in such wonderment at the return of his voice that he burst into prophetic song:

Blessed be the Lord, the God of Israel,
Because he has visited and brought redemption to his people.
You, my child John ben Zacharias, will be called the prophet of the Most High,
Because it is you who will go before the Lord to prepare his way.
You will open the minds and hearts of his people,
Announcing to them his coming, and preaching to them forgiveness of their sins.
Oh you doubting men and women in my Temple,
Hear me now as I again address my infant son.
John ben Zacharias, we know of your vital role in the scheme of the Redemption.
The portent is nigh.
John ben Zacharias, my son, we follow your ways.
We trust your leadership of our people.
We send blessings to your work in the mountains and in the deserts and in the rivers.
We flock to your mighty hand as you baptize us in the name of the Lord.

Power. The worshipers admired greatly what they were witnessing and could not wait to tell their neighbors of what they had observed. They knew God had destined this child for something special, so they kept all that happened in their hearts to see how the child would grow and mature. They waited to see if John would fulfill Zacharias' prophecy.

The purple trim on Zacharias' robes radiated brilliantly when he made his announcement. The men in the crowd could not help but notice the power and authority by which he spoke. All men quivered behind their beards from the power he exuded in his voice. His voice shook the walls. All knew what he stood for; all present held him in the highest esteem. His voice was rich, vibrant, and strong, all the while giving purpose to the announcement he intended. He and the entire crowd could feel the unity with the higher self that was forming within them.

Everyone there knew that Zacharias had true dominion over his thoughts and feelings. Elizabeth shared her love for him by thinking caring thoughts for him.

CHAPTER 4

Autumn 8 BCE

Mary and Gabriel

The morning was cool. The farmers had ingathered their crops and the shepherds had penned their herds for the winter. Joseph and Mary had met to share their morning meal of lentil pottage and dried figs when Mary began a conversation.

"Something happened to me yesterday in the afternoon. I had to sleep with it last night and this morning to know that it was real and personal. The images have not gone away. Joseph, it really did happen."

"What was it?" He sensed that his best friend was about to reveal her innermost thoughts.

"I was frightened, truly, when it happened, oh Joseph," whimpered Mary.

"Do not be afraid to tell me," coaxed Joseph, holding her hand tenderly in his. "Go on, you can tell me everything as it happened."

"My lovely Joseph, you know we are betrothed, and we will marry one day; I would do nothing to tarnish our commitment." She breathed deeply and clutched her sewing unconsciously in her lap. "I dozed after tending to the morning chores, and I was in a state of half-sleep by the side of the low cypress table. It was as if I was dreaming, but not dreaming. I saw an apparition in my mind's eye. He was a beautiful and radiant man. I think he was an angel." Mary was uneasy in telling what she had seen.

"Go on, my dear," said Joseph.

"He—this divine herald—said to me, 'Hail, highly favored of God, the Lord is with you.' I was frightened, of course, and he saw that I was. He went on by saying, 'I am the angel Gabriel, a messenger of the Supreme Being. Do not be afraid, Mary, for you have found favor with God. You are blessed beyond all women. Behold, you will conceive and bear a son, and that conception within you shall be ordained by heaven. You shall name him Jesus. He will be great and will be called Son of the Most High, and the Lord will give him the throne of David. He will rule over the House of David forever. He will become a teacher of Truth to all races and all peoples. His kingdom will last forever. My benediction rests upon you and the power of the Most High will strengthen you. The Lord of all the earth shall overshadow you.'"

She continued in a confused whisper. "Of course I was afraid. Why should I, a country girl, be blessed beyond all women? Was I to be taken to a far off land to suffer or was I about to die? Did I violate the Jewish laws? And how can I bear a child since I have had no relations with you?"

Mary shifted on her stool. "I tried to look away from him because of the terror I felt. My eyes failed to move from Gabriel's; they were fixed to his. I knew vaguely that I was to become the mother of a king.

"There was more," she continued. "Gabriel's soft glow filled the room. He said to me, 'Woman, you will bear what the Jews have been awaiting for centuries. You will bear the Messiah, a Savior. He will be God come to earth as he promised long ago. Do you understand? The Holy Spirit will descend upon you and the power of the Most High will overshadow you. The child to be born will be holy, the Son of God. Know, too, that the Holy Spirit is the dynamic, living expression of God in all his potential. Doubt not my word, Mary, for your home has been chosen as the mortal habitat of the child of destiny.'"

"What did you do? What did you say?" was Joseph's only answer.

Gathering her confidence, she continued to relay Gabriel's words. "No, not me. Do not choose me. It cannot be me. I am not worthy. I am a modest woman leading a simple life." She paused to take in a deep breath. "Nevertheless, I shall be your humble servant."

Mary continued repeating Gabriel's words. "There is more. I feel you need reassurance of what you are about to undergo. To put your mind at rest, I will tell you a secret. Your cousin Elizabeth has also conceived a son in her old age, and she who was thought to be forever childless is already in her sixth month. She is no more barren. Nothing is impossible with God. She has more blessings now than the number of gray hairs on her head. My benediction rests upon you. The power of the Most High will strengthen you, and the Lord of the earth shall overshadow you."

Then Mary spoke her own words, releasing a great burden from her shoulders in so saying. "I felt *mechiah*, relief when he said that. I now feel a bond with my cousin whom I have not seen for some time. Imagine, she and I bearing children together. Is it not out of the ordinary that after all these years, she is ripe with child?"

"You should feel relieved, and I am glad for you," comforted Joseph, stroking her hand with his. "You are endowed with an enormous honor."

Mary continued speaking. "I said unto the angel, 'I feel assured now, beautiful one, that I am the handmaiden of the Lord. Let it be done to me according to your word.'"

"Yes. Go on."

"After I spoke these words," Mary continued, "the angel vanished as quietly as he had appeared, and I thought I had witnessed a dream. Only I knew it was not a dream, Joseph. It was real, very real, and I am pleased with God and myself for being chosen for this heavenly undertaking.

"I thought of telling my mother what I had seen. I decided against it because if the angel had wanted her to know, then he would have spoken to me when my mother was with me. He did not do that. Therefore, it is the will of God that I keep this secret until the time is right to reveal it; I know whom God selected for this honor. I will do my best to please God with my given task."

"You will do more than that, my beautiful friend," assured Joseph. "You will be holy in your own right. I know you will. You will perform your undertaking wonderfully. I am glad you told me of your vision."

Will. After the angel vanished, Mary had a fuller understanding of Gabriel's purpose. Mary knew now that the angel was her spiritual perceptive faculty, which ever dwelt in her inner consciousness. The angel projected a childlike facade, even though he understood and taught spiritual principles. His purpose was to guard, guide, and direct the natural forces of mind and body, which of course guard, guide, and direct the natural forces of all future humankind.

Mary continued. "Joseph, that angel who spoke to me floated down to me on silver wings. His brilliance inspired me to know my life's work and to perform it as God directs me. God's will is my will and I know it has only good results for me. I fear nothing, because I am willing to be God in expression. I allow it to be the opportunity through which the God-ness in me expresses my potential.

"Joseph, my dearest one, I want to become even closer to the Spirit than what I am now. I know the way to do that is to continue doing good works. You and I strengthen our spiritual character when we let God lead the way.

"The will of God is uppermost in my consciousness, and I am glorified in my understanding."

Joseph and Gabriel

Joseph stood up from his stool and stared out the window at the women carrying firewood on the lane. He gathered his courage and sat down. He continued the conversation. "I had a vision of my own. It was last night in my sleep."

"Please tell me of it," Mary encouraged.

"In my dream, an angel appeared before me. I, too, was frightened, but my angel was gentle with me and he said to me, 'Fear not, Joseph; I am Gabriel, a messenger of God. My pronouncement to you is clear. Take Mary your betrothed to be your wife, for the father of her child is the Spirit of God. Soon she shall give birth to a son, and you shall name him Jesus, and he shall be the Savior of his people.'

"There is more. My angel said, 'The son shall become a great glow unto the world. In him will be life and light, for light represents total understanding. He will appeal to his own people, but many of them will reject him. Others will follow him judiciously and will spread the great word of his life and teachings. People of all races and all beliefs in all lands will know him and love him. You, Joseph, are to do your part as the earthly father. You are to love this child. You are to teach him the laws of the Jews. You are not to hold fear in your heart for this occasion, for God loves you. You know what you must do. You will do it well. Go, and be at peace.'

"I received from my angel the same message you received from your angel, my dearest," said Joseph quietly. "I am sure my seraph was the same

Gabriel as your angel. Is not our God a truly great God, for he provides for us true confirmation of that which is about to happen? I am greatly blessed to know you and love you, my Mary. I love you even more than before and I shall be honored to wed you."

"Bless you, Joseph. I love you, too."

They moved to a corner of the room and gave each other a warm hug. Joseph continued their conversation as they hugged each other. "I feel that the messages we received give us truly deep blessings. We are truly blessed. We are blessed."

Even after their hug, Joseph still felt a little uneasy at the prospect of becoming a new father. He still held reservations in the back of his mind as to how two common citizens would become the earthly parents of the Messiah. How could the offspring of human beings be a child of divine destiny? How would the world change after the birth? He had many unanswered questions in his mind.

CHAPTER 5

Early 7 BCE

Mary Travels

A few weeks after Gabriel visited her, Mary asked her parents, as casually as possible, for permission to visit her cousin Elizabeth. Mary wanted to visit with her and her husband Zacharias. Her mother thought it was a touching sign of devotion. Mary's secret was still her secret from her mother. Joseph understood her need to go. I was pleased to see Mary comfortable in her new role.

Four miles west of our large city of Jerusalem, and ninety miles south of Nazareth, is a small village named Ain-Karem. That is where Elizabeth lived.

"Joseph, my love," said Mary, "I feel compelled to travel south to visit my cousin. I know it is an arduous journey, but I feel the need to go. I must visit Elizabeth. You do understand my need, do you not, Joseph?"

"Indeed I do. Go in peace," said Joseph. "Be safe in your journey. I will await you here."

"Joseph, dear, I travel not alone, for there happens to be a caravan of merchants traveling south at the same time as I travel. It seems the caravan is nearly a daily event." Mary adjusted her basket on the camel. "I can travel in comfort because Chaim's friend Uri is traveling that way. He is able to let me ride on his unused camel for the three-day journey."

"*Nesi'a tova.* Go with God, my love." Joseph wished her good journey.

Uri, whose name means, "Giver of the Light," is my friend who lives near Ain-Karem. He tells me of everyday activities that go on in and around Jerusalem. The first thing I ever learned about Jerusalem, when I was a boy, is that the word means, "Dwelling Place of Peace." As I have grown older, I have come to understand its deeper meaning—that Jerusalem is a sacred place that abides in spiritual peace.

Mary Visits Elizabeth

My intuition was great; I knew when Mary arrived in Ain-Karem. When she arrived there, Mary was not weary from the road, and so approached Elizabeth's house enthusiastically. Elizabeth was standing, waiting in the doorway, having seen Mary approaching the gate from the road. Mary, being excited, shouted a greeting to Elizabeth before reaching the door. "Hello, my dearest cousin Elizabeth. Shalom to you and your baby! I arrive from Nazareth."

The baby inside Elizabeth's womb was no ordinary infant. He was unusually perceptive and intelligent. When he heard Mary's cheerful voice, he inspired Elizabeth to sing out:

> Mary, dearest child of God's good,
> With your precious babe inside.
> You would visit me to lift my spirit!
> Your words fill me with much delight;
> The music of your voice kisses my ears.
> The womb-ed infant inside me kicks with joy
> To fill the prophecy by you, oh peerless one!

"Elizabeth!" cried Mary, "Are you suggesting that I am expecting? How did you know of my vision of the angel?" She now knew that she was indeed the chosen woman to deliver the Savior to the world. She no longer worried about her part in God's will.

"Yes, child," comforted Elizabeth, "I know you are with a splendid gift. And I know that your Joseph knows of this. He is grateful and he appreciates this wonderful event."

Then Mary burst into her own poetic cry:

> My soul proclaims the greatness of the Lord,

And my spirit rejoices in God my Savior.

He has looked upon the lowliness of me, his handmaid Mary.

From now on, all ages will call me blessed,

For he who is mighty has done great things for me, and holy is his name.

"Mary, my child, slow your words," reproved Elizabeth. "You are with me in my home and you need not be so exuberant with this blessed event. I bless you and love you just the way you are."

"I cannot restrain myself," continued Mary. "From generation to generation is God's mercy to those who revere him. God shows his great strength, scattering the wicked in their pride. He dethrones the mighty and exalts the lowly. The rich he dispossesses. He strengthens his servant Israel, ever mindful of his past mercy, as he has promised to our father Abraham and to his descendants forever."

"Bless you, my dear cousin. You are blessed. I am grateful that you chose to come visit me while I am with child," thanked Elizabeth. "I will make your stay here most comfortable."

Mary smiled. "Look at you, dear Elizabeth. Your belly is big as a melon. Be proud of yourself, as Zacharias is proud of you. God is with us; God is good."

The women embraced and had a warm visit. After two months, Mary returned to her own home with a sincere heart, knowing that she had been truly helpful to Elizabeth.

On the road north, Mary again traveled in Uri's caravan. Conversation helped to pass the trip all too quickly. To allow herself brief diversions while the others rested, she wandered off the road into the hillsides and the ravines to search for useful herbs. Any plant part was potential—leaves, stems, roots, blossoms, fruits, and barks. She was wise enough to know helpful herbs from poisonous herbs. From her mother she had learned how to dry them, crush them, boil them, or make a paste of them, each according to the medicinal properties hidden within. She would always be grateful to her mother for teaching her the natural remedies.

Shortly after Mary reached her home, Elizabeth gave birth to her son.

CHAPTER 6

Spring 7 BCE

Another Angel

After Mary returned to her home, Joseph went to her house and welcomed her with open arms and warm hugs. He noticed that she had changed somehow. He noticed that she was more vibrant and more alive. He noticed that her demeanor issued a glow deep from within, and he knew why.

It was after Joseph noticed the change in Mary's deportment that he made a decision. He decided that they would tell their parents and some of their friends of the miracle that had happened to them. They did not tell everyone, but only those who would believe the words they would tell them. They knew that by telling a few select friends, that eventually the message would trickle out into the village that Mary was with child and the circumstances surrounding the miraculous conception. Too, by telling only select friends of their marvelous occasion, that would prevent any unkind rumor or gossip from spreading through the village.

Later that day, Joseph's mind drifted to the memory of Gabriel's visits. He remembered the dream he had one night before Mary left on her trip. He remembered her dream, too, in which she described so vividly how she was to become the mother of Jesus. He was proud that Mary was with child. He was proud that she had conceived a son who was to become the Savior named Jesus. Most of all, he was proud to be the earthly father for Jesus. The fact that he had taken the vows at the Kidushin ceremony finalized everything.

He breathed deeply and prayed a quiet prayer to thank God for his understanding and for Mary's safe return.

After uttering his prayer, a strange thing happened. Another angel whispered into his ear. Again he was startled, for he thought he had finished talking with angels. "Joseph, I come to remind you of the meaning of Jesus' name. The name Jesus conveys God's idea of man in expression. Jesus is that idea in the absolute. Jesus is the spiritual awareness in each man, as experienced by each man in his own way. Jesus is the mind of God. Jesus is a perfect being, as is the God in heaven. In a deep sense the word Jesus means, 'God with Us.'"

The silence was sudden. When the angel finished whispering his message to Joseph, he vanished as quietly as a candle smoldering into the night, leaving Joseph unable to move or speak for many minutes. He was in a good stupor. He knew the name Jesus was the perfect name for the new baby.

Understanding. He felt content in his love for Mary.

The golden sunset that day allowed Joseph to understand his complex relationship with Mary. Their love was an easy love, as easy as the morning mist. Their love was rooted in their youth by having grown up on the same side of the village, only five lanes apart from each other—hardly a three-minute walk.

They saw the light glowing in each other, the radiance of their being when they passed in the market or when they saw each other on the Sabbath. They knew there was some strange and vague force cultivating between them, something that neither could identify. Each of them would not let that feeling go away. It was yawning, crying out to be recognized—to become open and free and uninhibited. It had to happen; it needed to happen; it was required. That unnamed something was unstoppable. It had no boundaries. Their love for each other was deep and strong, even though they did not know it when they were young. They were too busy living and performing their chores to recognize the role that they would become to each other as adults.

And now that they were adults and betrothed, his love for her was easy to understand. It was in the light of the Spirit. He understood how the laws of thoughts and ideas brought him, and all men, closer to comprehending God and God's laws. Loving Mary gave him all the proof he needed to know God was with him always and in all ways.

Divine understanding unites us with the God-Spirit, and we always know what to do because God stands under all things.

Joseph's Confession

One day while Mary was weaving a shawl on her loom, Joseph approached her and massaged her shoulders. "Mary, my love, I must tell you something that is on my mind."

She stopped the shuttle's progress and held it in her hand while she turned around to look up at him. "Yes, my dearest, what is it?"

"I must tell you of my unease when you went away to visit Elizabeth. I was sad that you felt you had to go for such a long time. I was lonely for you. I missed you. I wanted you to be here with me or me with you; it did not matter. I wanted to see your face, your sparkling eyes and your hair brushed soft the way I like it. I wanted to touch you, to hold your hand, to whisper to you that I love you. I wanted all of these things to happen when you were away. I was quiet with myself.

"It was my work that kept me going. I have so many jobs to do here in Nazareth and nearby that on some days, truthfully, I did not think of you all that much. But there were times when I did—and it was hard. Another way I kept myself occupied was to search for a home where we may live after we marry. I located some and they are good, but they will have to wait until after we are wed. I am grateful now because you are here, back with me, back in our village where we both belong." He hesitated, thinking of how to say what was to come next. "Mary, thank you for being my friend. I love you. I love our baby."

"Oh, Joseph, my Joseph, I am so glad you want to be with me. Thank you for loving me and my little baby inside." She caressed her belly. "I adore you, Joseph."

"Mary, my sincerest friend," Joseph said quietly, "I will stand beside you with what you are about to bear. Your burden will be great and it will be splendid at the same time. You will have the world look upon you as you go about presenting us with the little one known as Jesus. You will be a proud mother and a loving one, I know. Our little baby will be the pride of Nazareth, you wait and see. When your time comes to deliver, you will not be alone; I promise that to you. I will be with you whenever you need my help. And I will help you."

Joseph felt refreshed; he was happy and renewed because of what was about to unfold before his eyes. The Scripture said plainly that the Messiah would be born of a virgin. He sensed and he knew that because of the virgin birth, he and Mary would not burden Jesus with any unnecessary emotional burden. He could and would grow up as a normal boy as much as possible for as long as possible. He promised himself that he would oblige himself and Mary to work very diligently to achieve this goal.

I saw that something troubled Joseph. Everyone knew that the sacred Scriptures said that the King of Kings would be born in Bethlehem, the City of David. He knew otherwise—he just *knew* it—that their infant son would be born right here in our own village of Nazareth. To travel ninety miles in Mary's advanced condition to deliver a baby was out of the question. Neither of them intended to travel anywhere, especially such a long distance, especially as Mary approached her delivery.

Thinking of such a trip perplexed Joseph. He had better things to do than to imagine such a trip. He had daily chores—he was a busy man! The more he thought about the fictional trip, even unconsciously as he worked his trade, the more he came to understand the significance it would shed on their lives, assuming of course that it ever took place. He remembered the lessons his father had taught him when he was a young boy. It was during an afternoon walk in a nearby vineyard when his father had told him about the meaning of the word David.

Joseph remembered. *I know the word David means, "Divine love individualized in human consciousness." I know that David is a mere forerunner of the perfect man Jesus, whom my Mary is to deliver soon. I respect the laws laid down before my time and know that David is our ancestor, whom we adore. I accept what is to be.*

As her parents and the town women noticed Mary's waist grow large, they counseled her to remain close to her home. She would not travel to see Elizabeth's baby, so why should she travel to Bethlehem? Joseph agreed wholeheartedly and that was the end of that discussion. He had never been to Bethlehem and he was not about to go there now.

While Joseph waited for Mary's time to arrive, he kept himself busy with his chosen trade. I was proud of how he kept his mind and hands occupied. Daily, he found work that only skilled carpenters like himself could perform, such as finishing interior decorations and building fine furniture. When he had no such work, he worked beside my coworkers and me as we constructed new homes for our expanding populace. It was during those times that I was able to talk with him so freely.

Why Carpentry?

I knew there were times when Joseph had second thoughts about choosing the profession he did. A carpenter of all things—what was he thinking? The truth was that he had no thinking to do because he knew nothing else. His father and his father's father before him both heeded the same call. And now, Joseph, too, yielded to the lure of his tools. Of all of the ways to earn his existence, woodworking was one of the hardest. Generations had passed down the best tools to him and he had become proficient in their use. He knew that he would pass down those same tools to his son.

It was a demanding business, carpentry. Joseph tried his best to be good at it. He made mistakes in calculating and measuring, and cutting the wood, too. Some days he wasted nearly as much wood as he used. He knew he was not perfect. *Who was perfect?* Joseph wondered half aloud. What made his work difficult was getting the wood. Fig trees, date palms, and pomegranates grew plentifully, but fruit trees were not intended for furniture. The woods he preferred—sycamore and oak—were expensive because they came from Lebanon and Syria with the camel caravans. He knew that beautiful groves of cedar trees grew in the mountains of Lebanon to the north. He worked mostly in pine and cypress. He took what he could get.

Joseph made yokes for the oxen and plows for the farmers. He made threshing boards, boxes, assorted tools, lattices for the vines, and furniture. His favorite work, however, was to build a cart, its axle, and two wheels because they were creative and filled up many hours of honest labor. Besides, he could demand a good wage in exchange for his talent. The variety of work kept him satisfied.

When he had not these opportunities, he worked instead with me to build houses. He had to provide the beams for the roof. Sometimes, a house would have beam supports up the walls. A carpenter sculpted the lintels above the doorframes and the windows, too. Those were his everyday jobs.

It was one evening as we walked to our homes that Joseph began a conversation about his carpentry business. "Chaim, there is something that is on my mind and I must say it aloud. When I say that I make a stool from a tree, something is missing from those words. I cannot just shave the bark from the tree and call it a stool. I feel a deeper connection to the wood than merely changing its shape. Who made the tree? God made the tree. All I can do is carve the wood until it looks like a stool. Do you understand what I say? When I say that I make a lattice for Mary's cucumber vines, I know deep within my being that I cannot make a lattice from a tree. I cannot make a box from a tree. I cannot make an ox's cart from a tree. After all, did I make the tree? Did I create the tree?"

I scratched my beard and frowned. "I am not sure of your meaning, Joseph. Say it again."

"When Mary says that she makes the evening meal, does she really make the evening meal? In a deep sense, she does not. When a cooper builds a barrel, does he really build a barrel? In a deep sense, he does not. They take what God gave to them and change it into another form. Only God can create. Only God can make. Mary can prepare a meal; she cannot make a meal. Mary can bake a loaf; she cannot make a loaf."

It was my turn to speak. "I am beginning to understand your meaning. Let me say it aloud for myself." I studied his face against the sunset. "You are saying that because only God can create anything, then we cannot create. All we can do is change what is already at hand. Yes, I think I know what you say."

Joseph nodded his head silently and smiled.

The Old Olive Tree

Ach! None of that mattered now. Joseph was experienced at age eighteen and had his own business in the village. He had his own clientele and a circle of people who came to him for his kind of work. He could not and dared not look backward and begin again in another trade. Too, he had to know that many families made their own accessories for their homes, thus depriving Joseph of his own trade.

I have known Joseph since he was a boy. He and I have traveled the roads around Nazareth in the course of our daily lives. Indeed, for his age, he is very skillful and resourceful in his trade. I have seen him look in discarded piles of rubble searching for wood. He is not a man of means and he uses whatever materials he can acquire. Sometimes when he finds a job, his client provides the materials he needs for the job, but usually it is up to Joseph to provide whatever is required to finish the task he is assigned. And he does finish every task in a proper timeframe and within the cost he promised to the buyer of his craft.

Sabbath days were special for Joseph, for it was on that day that he did not have to consider his daily labor. Being a good Jew, he knew that the Sabbath gave him a state of mind that led him to a precious silence all his own. He had fulfilled the divine law in both thought and in act, and now he could rest, knowing he had performed well on his duties of the week.

On Sabbath days, after he had fulfilled his prescriptions according to the law, Joseph would often walk to the old olive grove outside of Nazareth. He had heard of a magnificent grove of olive trees in Jerusalem called the Mount of Olives and he knew that everything in and around Jerusalem had to be superior to anything, anywhere else. Nevertheless, he cherished this grove, so close to his home, for it had in its center a magnificent old tree that rose skyward many times the height of a man. Its branches were twisted and gnarled, which only added to its personality. Joseph knew that this tree was a symbol of life and love, for it knew only how to grow and multiply and sprout forth fruit and green leaves each year. How gracious it was to share its strength, vitality of life, and ongoing robustness with each of us! Its vigor never failed to amaze Joseph in its ability to be, just be, what it was. Praises be to God for giving him a true example of the splendor of the world around him.

CHAPTER 7

Summer 7 BCE

~⌣⌣~

Galilee

I love Nazareth. Nazareth is a lesser village. It began as an oasis in the desert many centuries ago. Over the years, travelers found the oasis water to be pure and cold, and fashioned it into a vital water well amidst the fig trees and olive trees. Tents and then houses sprouted up around the oasis.

Most streets within are not much more than graveled pathways and many are not in a straight line. Very little is of marble or stone, nothing is artfully aesthetic, and certainly no building displays mosaics or frescoes on the outside. Any hint of beauty is reserved for the insides of the rooms where my fellow citizens appreciate the beauty more fully. The winery, the grain industry, and the pottery factory each flourish in their own way.

My Nazareth is situated inside the area called Galilee.

Galilee is a mix of Jews and Gentiles. History places it central among feuding tribes and warring peoples. Trade routes to distant lands and camels laden with grains, olive oil, wines, fruits, nuts, dates, and fish crisscross the territory. Galilee has no capital city of its own, no king, no temple, and no hierarchy of priests. Some of us Jews call it, as it means, "The Land of the *Goyish*, The Land of the Gentiles." Galilee is my home. To experience Galilee is to experience life and energy.

The history of Galilee is long and notable. Every day that passes adds richness to my heritage. Oh! That I might live more years so I could see and touch and smell the daily stories happening right now, right here, every day. How blessed I am that I recognize the import of it all; how blessed I am that I recognize the great role our leaders fill. I am blessed, too, to have the skill to talk about ordinary events that might otherwise go unrecorded on scrolls or on tablets. I feel important in my village in that I can fill a role of oral historian and fill it well. I hope that my contribution to the Jewish tradition of oral history is great.

The Census

Our people have a brutal history of foreign rulers. We have known nothing but subjugation by foreigners for thousands of years. Those foreigners, then and now, spread over us like bees protecting their queen. There were Egyptians, Assyrians, Babylonians, Persians, and Greeks. And now there are the Romans. Our lands were desecrated over and over again. All we could do as a society was to hold our collective breath and be brave into the future, whatever it would bring.

History shows that the Romans were generous with our religious freedom, in that they allowed us to practice our Judaism. Too, they allowed us a limited amount of political freedom and thought, so long as we did not overstep their Roman-defined boundaries. For example, we were under our own Jewish court system, the Sanhedrin, yet all rulings for the death penalty were sent to the Roman government. Those things stand true today.

Recently in Rome, the emperor Caesar Augustus learned that many of his subjects were dishonest. He ruled the known world, at least the world he knew. He knew that the amount of taxes flowing into his hands was not in measure with the number of subjects. His advisors told him that he could levy an equitable tax on his populations, but first he had to learn the numbers of those populations in all of his provinces.

Because he had no religion, Caesar subscribed to the idea that every religion was trite and of little consequence to peoples' daily lives. His only concern was amassing wealth and influence over as much territory as practical. Because we Jews have been the subject of enormous prejudice and injustice for centuries before his time, he considered us to be a disposable minority. Therefore, as far as Caesar was concerned, every Jew was dishonest; every Jew was a threat to his power.

My friends tell me I talk too much. But there is so much to say, I cannot quiet my mind or my mouth.

Caesar disappointed me. He issued a proclamation to all of his subjects in all of his lands. Each citizen was to return to the city of his father and there, be numbered. Such an unwise decree surely damaged the Roman nation during the appointed time because men had to leave their employ and not earn their wages. The marketplaces did not sell the fruits, the leathers, or the baskets. The chickens, the tools, and the sandals all had to wait. Ach! The folly of it all! The census was taken in many tongues and on many shores. Galilee was no exception.

It had to be done.

"The census is indeed a burden on everyone!" Joseph, in a rare episode of frustration, raised his voice and shouted into the air. His saw clattered to the ground, startling the donkey. "Caesar, leave us alone so that we may go about our daily lives and earn our daily bread. We know how to live our own lives in Nazareth.

"You know not what is involved in such an undertaking because you are an isolated leader and know not the ways of us, the workers and the toilers, those of us who actually fulfill the decree; you want only tax takings."

Being of the House of David, both Joseph and Mary had to travel to our capital Jerusalem, in the southern part of Judea.

The name Judea is the source word for the meaning of "Jew." When I say the words "House of David," I refer to the village where their ancestor and mine, King David, was born and where he lived.

When the betrothed pair first learned of the requirement that they had to travel, they were displeased, as was I and everyone else. Joseph did not stand by idly. He and others searched out the local tax merchant and asked if women in advanced pregnancy might be excused. Others asked about the lame, the blind, the lepers. The answer was, "All must enroll. No one is excused. All must travel."

Acceptance

"A long journey is not what we need right now," said Joseph worriedly. "How will you endure such a long trip in your condition? You are delicate."

"Do not fear," replied Mary. "I will be just fine, my love. I am not as tender as I look. True, I am more than eight months along and I should not be about such a trip right now, but I will be fine. I know I will. I need to prepare my mind, and then my body and our little one inside will be safe. Those miles will pass smoothly."

"Oh, Mary, you are always the optimist," answered Joseph. "Maybe that is why I love you so much."

"And I love you too, my sweet Joseph. Do not ever forget that." Mary stood and massaged her hips with her hands. "Maybe our son will wait until we arrive home after the census. He has been such a good little one so far. For all these months, he has been a real angel inside of me; he has not hurt me in any way. Besides, if he decides it is time to become known, I think we are prepared for it. After all, Joseph, we are a hardy pair, do you not think? You and I have been through many good and difficult times growing up together. A little adventure never hurt anyone. As I think, this possibly may be a perfect time to visit my kinswoman Elizabeth and her new baby."

"As usual, my love, you are right," said Joseph thoughtfully. "We can and we will make this trek meaningful. Let us be grateful for this challenge. Let us be safe." He paused to scratch his beard and think. "We need to gather a few items for our trip. I will set to it."

He looked around the room for the belongings they needed for the trip, and said, "Being with other travelers will lighten the load on us. I can walk and you can ride our donkey. It is likely that nobody will even notice us being with them, other than our friends, as there are so many travelers. As long as we travel with those we know from Nazareth, we will be inconspicuous, as a leaf in a bowl of olives. We want to remain unnoticed to protect you, my love, and our baby. All of our intentions from now on must be to keep Jesus safe. It is our duty to do that. We want to draw no attention to your delicate condition if we can. When we meet people we know, we will be pleasant to them. Mary, I love you and we will have a safe journey."

I do not have to worry about what to say or what to do because he who sent me will direct me.

CHAPTER 8

Summer 7 BCE

South of Nazareth

"This road we travel! It is so congested! The dust and the din of noise on the road are alarming." Joseph seemed exasperated, as well he should. "Look at those Greeks, how they flaunt their wealth. Look, they travel south and travel north to trade with the rich Jews scattered around Judea, Samaria, and Galilee. Mary, do you see those burdened servants of the Greeks, shouldering those sedan chairs, carrying their masters?"

"I do," said Mary. "I see all of them. The scene is a discord of dust and dirt. This time of census makes the road busy from early morning until the sun goes down."

"Look, look over there." Joseph pointed a finger. "Look how their robes seem to float on air and their useless decorations make clatter with every step. The Greeks and especially the Romans do almost anything to throw insult upon us. We must continue to be tolerant of their behavior."

Other travelers on the road from Jerusalem to Galilee were, as often as not, Egyptian merchants laden with fabrics and metal objects and expensive spices. Having wealth strapped over their camels allowed them the arrogance to wish "Fair day!" to those traveling in the opposite direction, as cavalierly as calling for a sip of wine of their servant.

"Joseph, I trust what you say. I have always and I will always trust you, because you are my unafraid husband and leader." Mary stiffened her shoulders and massaged her swollen belly gently. "I know we will be safe and our baby will be safe, too. I can almost feel his aura surrounding my belly. Some days, my womb tingles with his beaming love. It is a wonderful feeling inside my mind to know that the Savior will be born of me. I cannot thank God enough for that privilege."

"Rest, love. Just rest."

It was my privilege to travel with Joseph and Mary. Like them, my lineage is of the House of David, and therefore I too must travel so that I may be numbered. I am blessed richly with their friendship. Praises be to God.

Now I can almost see Joseph's mind mulling our situation. I can almost hear what he is thinking next. *Traveling fulfills the ancient prophets' words. That is true. Another idea I have is that a long and arduous journey might risk the life and safety of the baby. I dare not tell that to Mary aloud. On second thought, how unreasonable that thought is because if the baby were indeed the Messiah, then no harm can come to him.*

Conversation

The pair and I left Nazareth on the main road that pointed down through Nain and on into the valley of the Jordan. It was hot along the valley floor, as I can attest, but suffering in the hotness was far preferable to taking the upland country and the direct route. The upland road through Samaria and Sychar could mean risking life and possessions, as the inhabitants there were often unfriendly and quarrelsome with strangers traveling on their roads.

By dusk of the first night, we reached the southern foothills of Mount Gilboa. We could see the Jordan Valley to the east and the road we had just traveled to the north. We knew that Samaria was to our south and our destination even farther south. To pass the idle time, Mary and Joseph engaged in speculations as to what sort of a man their son would grow to become. I listened intently.

"He will become a wonderful and sage spiritual leader of our people," Joseph asserted. "What else could he become? He will be a strong organizer of our many tribes. I will instruct him in the laws and governance of the Jewish people. I will nurture him suitably. He will receive a proper education."

"Yes, that is true," assured Mary, remembering her conversation with Gabriel. "But I see that he will be more than that. He will rise to be a true Jewish Messiah, the one prophesized in the Scriptures. He will be the one to deliver our Hebrew nation to freedom—freedom of thought and of worship. He will become known throughout the lands farther away than we can imagine. He is the anointed one. He will show all of humankind how to search for and find the true soul within each of us—to pour out the spirit of love on one who has faith in God. He will teach us of God's Light that dwells within each one of us. We can find the presence of God in the midst of all humanity; it is in each experience, in each conversation, and in each task. We are God's eyes, heart, and arms in expression. Remember that."

They had been through these conversations many times in the past, but tonight's deliberation carried more meaning because we were on the road to the capital city. We were pilgrims; they were adventurers to unseen territory, as I had been to Jerusalem in the past. Every sight, smell, and sound resounded and remained in their minds with great lucidity. Mary's youthful spirit kept their strength high.

I could sense that the two shared a deep spiritual bond. I know they did. Indeed, they were meant for each other. I overheard a conversation they shared one evening. Joseph began. "Mary, what do you think it means to have a consciousness? What I mean to ask is this. Do you think all of humanity has a consciousness—that awareness or realization of something bigger than anything we can define?"

"Of course, wise man of mine. Why do you ask me such a question when I know perfectly that you know the answer to your own question?"

"Yes I do, Mary. I believe that consciousness—a system of ethics—is to know what we know; it is to recognize what we recognize. To have consciousness is to understand our relationship to the world around us, that which we can see and touch and smell with our physical senses. It means, too, that those ideas of what we sense around us—what we hold in mind—are the basis for all knowing. What we hold in mind is what manifests into our daily lives."

"Go on."

"If we have consciousness of eternal life, than we are in the stream of life that never fails. Without such an awareness of eternal life, then spirit, soul, and body will be separated. The ultimate in knowing is to know the Divine Mind and its laws."

Mary turned and studied his face. "I love you."

Joseph had to finish his thought. "In addition to each of us having an individual consciousness, we, collectively, have a universal and all-encompassing consciousness. I mean, there is all around and within us an ever-expanding Deity-consciousness of divine love. Divine love belongs to all of us."

He could not see the faint smile of contentment on Mary's face.

Quietness crept over both of them. It was dark now. They reached for each other's hand and stood quietly, looking down into the remaining light that defined the Jordan Valley.

Two more days of travel passed. The couple slept in the open each night, under the blackness of their celestial umbrella. This night, it was especially dark, as the moon did not appear. One skin Joseph had brought was filled with olive oil. That oil fueled the lamp and sweetened their food, that is to say, a little barley bread and some raisins and fruits. Their friends who worked the olive orchards made sure they had a full flask of oil before they set out on their trip. Mary had used what spare grain she had to make extra loaves before they began the trip. They ate lamb seldom. Mayhap one meal a week they would eat diced lamb cooked in oil and mixed with herbs. Fish they ate more often. In their pouch, they carried a small quantity of mandrake root to be used to bring sleep if necessary.

A Precious Oil

Mary knew the effort involved in making the valuable olive oil. Her friends in the village had told her how it was made. The olives, upon reaching ripeness, were plucked into baskets. Then maids cored out the pits with simple knives. They placed the olive meats into a vat where they pressed down on it with a large flat stone. For larger quantities, they fed the pitted olives through an ox-powered mill. Soon, in either case, they had a quantity of oil. Other oils were available, of course, like flaxseed oil and grape seed oil, but none matched the superiority and versatility of the oil from olives. Overall, the oil of olives is the most precious of all oils. She remembered many ceremonies from her girlhood that used olive oil as an ointment. How could she forget her betrothal ceremony? She knew that to anoint meant to rub the skin with oil. It was through massaging of the skin that sent the spirit of life into the body's awareness.

The best of the olive oil was used for burning in lamps, for making soaps, and for anointing and massaging oneself or others. The oil for anointing was mixed with spices and it was pleasing to feel on any skin. Olive oil was stored in an earthenware vessel called an asak; the container was high and narrow. The top was stoppered with a piece of carved soft wood as a plug. To hold the vessels upright, they were placed into a stone hewn with a hole for that very purpose or into a wooden stand. Often, they were buried in the ground. They had no handles. I saw a creative goat herder one time with a leather strap crafted for the very purpose of carrying his asak.

Refreshment

Joseph nursed the lamp of its minimum light so that Mary could remove her veil and prepare for sleep. She brushed her long dark hair, which when unfurled, hung to her waist. Every time Joseph saw Mary with her hair hanging loose, he thought to himself, *what a handsome woman you are! I am blessed to be such a privileged man. You will make a fine mother.*

Mary wished that she could bathe in the river. "Joseph, it would be so refreshing for me to wash myself of the dust. Come with me to watch over me while I cleanse myself."

"I want to disallow you, because as you know, it would not be proper for a woman to expose even a little of herself to the openness. However, I, too am dirty to the bone and welcome a splash in the river, so I will allow you to go. I must go with you. We must be quick. Take this cloth and use it to sponge yourself clean. If you desire, I will help you to wash your back."

"Thank you. It will feel refreshing to feel coolness on my skin," said Mary. "I know that our baby will appreciate its coolness, too."

"We are fortunate that the emperor Caesar did not order the census during the chill months of winter. The winds and rains would make us miserable."

"Indeed they would."

"There are those of us Jews who are volatile enough that if they had to travel in winter, they may have rebelled openly against Caesar," Joseph continued. "I think that Caesar would not want to put down such an uprising in cold weather."

"Again, Joseph, you make such good arguments for common sense. You are a good man." Mary did not know in-depth of the politics of the regions as deeply as did Joseph, but she was always learning something of value through Joseph's discourse with her. "You make me happy."

The Jordan River felt cool and delicious on their road-weary bodies, if only for a little while. They lingered not long at the river. In the near-distant darkness they could see the night fires of other pilgrims and see the shadows of men sitting and arguing, sometimes in Greek and sometimes in Aramaic.

The next morning, the fourth morning, Joseph arose, adjusted his tunic and mantle, and went about his chores of brushing and feeding the animal, allowing Mary to sleep while she could. He set the worn blanket on the donkey's back, knowing that Mary had already become accustomed to its coarseness. Joseph was gentle to the only donkey they owned, for he knew that it secured his livelihood in ordinary times. He cooed to the animal, much as Mary talked to him, calming him before the start of the day. He adjusted the goatskins containing the water and the foods over his back, making sure that all was well and proper for the next leg of their journey. Joseph recognized that the precious water represented all of the changing conditions in Mary's and his lives. Water gave cleansing and vital energy to each person and every living thing.

I prepared my pack of meager belongings and made ready to walk with them.

That day would see us to the outskirts of Bethany. "Mary, wake. We need depart. We have another day of travel before we reach our destination. We must press on. We still have twenty miles to Bethany. Finally, from Bethany, we trek west a mere two miles to Jerusalem—our journey's end. We can make it to there this day before the sun goes down."

"Good morning and God's morning. I will be ready in a minute," yawned Mary. "I slept well last night. I feel rested and ready for whatever this day may bring."

"It will be another warm day," answered Joseph. "We do not want to be left behind. We must keep up with others going south."

"Today is our third day of travel, is it not, my love?" asked Mary. "Even though I am rested, my legs are chafed from the swinging goatskins. My seat is sore and my shoulders ache. The dust and the countless pebbles are mere stepping stones on this journey. All I do is for the protection of our little one while we adhere to the law."

"No. This is the fourth day. This day we will arrive in Jerusalem. There, we can rest and nourish our bodies without having to test them to the limits. One more day of this travel and we can rest." Joseph was as anxious as Mary was to reach there.

The road out of Jericho led slowly out of the east toward the splendor of Jerusalem. Family by family, each group led their donkeys to their goal. The graceful feet of the animals gave the image of almost floating over the dust, except that by now, Joseph knew that they were not floating, but working, walking. Pilgrims came to Jerusalem all year long from Jericho and the Salt Sea, and indeed, from every direction. They came from the mountains of Moab and from the plains of Samaria and Galilee to see the Temple of Herod the Great. Arriving in Jerusalem was a great feat, almost a spiritual spawning—a communion with the great God in his own house. This time, however, the trek to the Temple felt more like work to those who had been there before, as now it was an obligation rather than a choice to see it.

Arrival at Jerusalem

Jerusalem! What a marvelous sight they were about to behold. "Look, love, look there!" exclaimed Joseph, pointing westward from the top of the rise. "Is it not wonderful? Praise God for giving us this privilege."

Mary's mild nausea faded when she looked up in the direction of Joseph's finger. Her eyes lost the glazed look. She had heard her father describe this place when she was a little girl. It was a sight to see, Jerusalem. The city was a white jewel encased in a great stone wall. Joseph jerked the donkey's rein to the side to allow shouting pilgrims to pass them. The animal was in no hurry. He took the pause to kick flies from his belly with his hind leg and to nibble a stray blade of weed in the rock.

I am as God created me.

Joseph's hand found Mary's. "Jerusalem, what a paradise it is. Let us savor this sight, for it is important for us to do so. Our fathers would want us to study this spectacle and remember it well, well into our old age. The light is fading. This is a special time for us."

Each of them longed to exclaim to each other the wonder they were witnessing. This is where God's Spirit lived. They had been told that many times in their youth. They had been told, too, that the Breath of God was not restricted to living in little synagogues around the country, but that God lived within their hearts. The synagogues were merely a reminder of their duties to worship God as best they could. They saw no contradiction in these two beliefs. Synagogue, in its meaning is, "House of Assembly." It is every Jew's duty to visit Jerusalem for the Passover whenever possible at the time of the Seder. Passover is sometimes called Pesach.

"We must continue. We must go. We have no time to waste." Joseph pulled the donkey into the road and trudged on. The closer to Jerusalem they drew, the more they saw of ox teams hauling large slabs of limestone to the incomplete Temple. In the morning, they would experience firsthand the noise and confusion of the construction, mixed so unceremoniously with the crying of the animals being slaughtered within. The rumors in the air told them that the Temple would be under construction for another several years beyond this time. The tradesman in Joseph allowed him to recognize the thousands of skilled masons and carpenters who milled around him. He learned through conversation with them that they were originally priests who had been trained in the trades by Herod. The priests were the only ones allowed to construct the Temple. The Temple was more than a mere construction. It was a device by which any man who entered into it could, if he wished, cleanse his mind, refresh his soul, and sanctify his spirit.

I have learned to know what is inside Mary's head. In her mind she was concentrating on what a beautiful baby she was about to deliver. She had seen other babies being born. After all, she had helped to midwife other women in their time of toil and ensuing joy, so she knew what to expect when her time arrived. She imagined when she would be able to hold the tiny one, to bathe him and to oil his skin. She marveled at the thought of holding his body against her uncovered breast to nurture him with the gift only a mother can give.

Her mind was an energetic mix of emotions. She was thinking of the many months leading up to this moment on this day. To have a baby, especially a first baby, was in and of itself a wondrous achievement. It was a wordless joy in the highest. But to give birth to the Son of God at a young age, now sixteen, was a heavier responsibility than any other woman had ever borne in the past. She knew the enormity of her task, and she was determined to do it to the best of her ability. She only hoped that one day she could look back and know she did her best.

The mother-to-be knew that God, her own personal and private God, was with her always. She knew that she must give to him the thanks he deserved. She knew this and she did pray quietly and constantly. Her breath swelled, as did her belly, with thanksgiving to her Guiding Light. She was happy knowing God and knowing that her God was with her always. The prayers floating from her lips made her happy. She was proud to know God so personally, as if she were the only one from Nazareth to pray. Alas, she was one of many, doing her godly duties daily. God should be pleased of her.

CHAPTER 9

Summer 7 BCE

Chaim's Lodging

On the way to our destination, I parted from Joseph and Mary to give them the privacy that any couple deserves to enjoy. I was content to have traveled this far with them and I knew they would be just fine on their own. On the road, I met three of my friends from Nazareth and we fell into conversation. We four were fortunate to find lodging in one of the public houses in Jerusalem because those three companions of mine had a way with words. They were able to convince the owner of a guesthouse to give us a room there.

The public house was small, too small for its purpose, and old. Old is a common word here because everything is old. In the center of the building was a hearth that blazed a wonderful fire. Arranged in front of it were a number of small tables, six I believe, and enough stools and chairs to accommodate the patrons. The floor and walls were of uneven wood. Lanterns hung on hooks from the beams in the ceiling to provide a dim light throughout. Above, up a crude ladder, were eight lodging rooms of very small size. My companions and I passed the night there.

The beds, as everything else, were of timeworn and splintering wooden planks, barely long enough to hold my frame, and not wide enough to allow a man's rolling over in the middle of the night. A series of discarded feedbags stuffed with hay comprised each mattress. I accepted my pallet gladly. It is a good thing I am in the habit of sleeping in my garments; otherwise, I would have itched the night through. One lantern was nailed to the wall and provided hardly enough light to see by, and it extinguished itself of fuel all too soon.

No Room in the Inn

Finding a fitting place to pass the night was futile, as it seemed no one would welcome Joseph and his weighted wife. It was not that the house owners and shop proprietors wanted to turn away trade; it was that they had no choice but to do so. From another public house, other than the one I stayed in, floated a distinct aroma of spicy foods and unwashed pilgrims into the evening air. That place is where the pair tried to attain a room for the night.

It was an ordinary looking place; it catered to transients like themselves. Stone was the main ingredient in its construction. Only small touches of wood decorated its trim. They peered into the doorway. The patrons took whatever food came from the kitchen; they had no choices. Food there, primarily watery lamb and chicken pottages, was steaming hot and arrived to the tables in tarnished and worn bowls. An occasional smaller bowl of mixed rice and vegetables added variety to the fare. "I will inquire inside," proffered Joseph.

Minutes later, he emerged. "This is not for us, for they will make us pay them more than we can rightfully give, assuming they have a place for us, which they do not. We cannot give to them what we have saved so diligently for the baby. Here in this place, the people are sleeping in turns in the same bed. Can you imagine? People are sleeping on the floor and in the barns. They are using their bundles as pillows. This census is causing us a lot of sorrow." He hesitated to issue a faint grimace of frustration across his face. "We must continue."

Mary, always the optimist, wanted to eat their evening meal and pass the night here, but her practical side agreed with her husband. Looking up from where she was resting on the house's stoop, she said, "Let us go."

Continuing, and with no intent of hiding his despair, Joseph said, "All of the houses are full. This abode is full. That abode is full. All abodes are full. The owner said so. The streets are full of families sleeping wherever they can. There is no room. I had no idea there were so many who belonged to the House of David."

They found another inn nearby. "Maybe the owner here can find us a place. Go inside and try again, my husband. I will wait for you to see if he can help us," said the ever-hopeful Mary. "If he cannot, we will find a place. God will provide. God always does."

Joseph was not inside long. "The owner said he would come to the door to speak to us because the clamor inside is too loud for conversation."

While he and Mary discussed their options, a figure appeared in the doorway. It was the proprietor. His apron was well-worn and torn, and not a little greasy. "I wish I could oblige you here, but there is no room. I have nothing," he shouted over the noise heaving from inside as he threw his hands up in despair. "There is no privacy anywhere. Even my own family has no privacy. Every cubit of space is full. Where can you sleep?—I know not where.

"The only thing I can think for you is that grotto that way out of town," the tavern-keep said, stabbing his finger into the darkness, "farther along, continuing south a short distance. It is near Bethlehem. An old woman and her husband keep animals in it. I know them. Maybe they will allow you to stay there. *Behatslacha*, shalom and good luck to you both."

"Thank you, friend. We will go there."

One more time, Joseph helped Mary to the top of the faithful beast. One more time, Joseph led Mary into the darkness to a place they knew not. One more time they kept the conviction that they would find a suitable place to rest, and if necessary, for the birth of their son.

Peace unto you, Mary, oh blessed mother of the Living Spirit. I love you for the work you are to undertake.

"Joseph, oh, no! No, not now! Joseph, my legs feel wet. I think my water has flowed from me. My time is very near. We must find a place." There was urgency in Mary's voice. "I feel cramps around my belly. The time is nigh. The hour is short." Her voice revealed streaks of panic.

"We will be fine, love. Try to remain relaxed," was all Joseph could think to say. He had no experience with babies being born. He had no idea what he was going to do. He was overwhelmed. *Perhaps I should have studied what to do with some of Mary's friends before we left*, he thought to himself. *How careless of me to think this would not have happened. How careless of me to not find a midwife at the tavern. I failed my duty as a husband*, he lamented to himself. *I must find a place for our baby. I must keep trying.*

The Woman of the Grotto

"This must be the cave the tavern-keep told us about," said Joseph, searching anxiously along the face of a steep hill. "Look, over there. See? Do you see it? The lantern shows a grotto."

They hurried to the blackness of the cave. In the faint glow of their lantern, Joseph saw a woman shooing her animals—three goats, four sheep, six thin cattle, and a young donkey—from the grotto into a makeshift corral of logs and rocks nearby.

"Are you the holder of this grotto?" Joseph asked of the woman, his arm around Mary's waist. "May we stay here for the night? My wife is due with child very soon, and the tavern is full."

"Of course. Our rulers told us to prepare this place for visitors, as were other shepherds in the area. They told us to accommodate the arrival of travelers. You came at the right time to my grotto. *Tuchal la'azor li*, help me to clean it up." She studied Mary and her belly. "You are tired, I can see that. Your bones must be weary. Bless you, my child; you need to rest. Come, let me help you."

Faith. The first thing Mary remembered of the woman was her penetrating dark blue eyes. After sensing the woman's genuine desire to help, Mary released all her uncertainty and with faith gave herself over to the woman. Mary said "Yes" to God and to Good.

Releasing herself to the woman's care allowed Mary to go within herself and to accept the spiritual faith residing there to do the things that needed to be done. She had complete confidence in the woman's skills because she discerned deep within her inner knowing that she, Mary, was in the right place at the right time and in the right care. The woman's gentle manner assured Mary that a miracle was about to happen.

Jesus Is Born

Joseph and the woman helped Mary from the animal and onto the ground. Then they worked at shoveling out the dirty hay and debris from the cave. Using clean hay, they lined the cattle's feeding trough as best they could to cover over the splinters, dried saliva, and mud. They pushed the salt cake to the end of the trough. Somehow, Joseph knew in his being that the manger signified that humankind would feed from this instance via the spiritual food in the manger—Jesus and his ministry. He knew, too, that this birth that was about to occur represented the rebirth of awareness of God's love. He knew that the rebirth of God's love embodied divine ideas such as intelligence, life, love, substance, and strength.

Mary had brought swaddles and Joseph's extra mantle, washed before leaving, in case this very event happened while they were there. She would use his mantle as a pillow for the baby, or maybe as an extra cover to keep him warm when the time came. She had thought of everything.

Mary was content to sit on the ground, with her back leaning against the dirt wall that held the crude wooden stalls. "Woman, what is your name? You are most kind to help us this way. I want to thank you."

"For you, I have no name," she replied, tightening the sash around her waist. "I am a mere sheep chaser's wife in the hills and I want nothing in return. Helping you is more than enough recognition for me. You are beginning your life and a new one, too. Mine is nearly at its end; all my needs are met."

Joseph had the presence of mind to leave the actual birthing to the women. To occupy himself, he led their donkey to be with the other animals in the corral. There, he built a small fire to heat the water from one of the goatskins. He had heard of other husbands boiling water at a time like this, but he was never quite sure of its purpose.

Blessed are those whose hearts are pure.

By now, other families had arrived near the grotto because, like Mary and Joseph, there was no room anywhere else for them to stay. By any standard, the cave was not big, nor was it comfortable or ventilated. It was a dreary place to spend the night, and certainly not a suitable place to deliver a baby. Out of respect for Mary's need for privacy, the other families stayed outside the grotto and made camp there for the night, near the logs and rocks that held the animals.

The animals sensed that this night was to be a special night. They have feelings and emotions, the same as people have feelings and emotions, only different. The difference between animals' emotions and human emotions is intensity. Creature emotions are gentler and kinder in so many ways compared to those in humans. Their feelings are only of love, affection, and fondness to each other and to their masters. They harbor no grudges or hold no bad memories. Mary knew that the animals in the corral would emanate only positive energies to the newborn babe.

Mary was thrilled to be at her task at last. If her son should be born in a place like this, she would not question the wisdom of it. The woman of the cave gave her full attention to Mary.

The woman produced from the depths of the cave two straps of leather, each three inches wide and about four feet long. Without uttering a word, she went to work to fashion one of the straps around Mary's upper arm to form a loop. She laced the ends together with sinew just out of reach of Mary's fist. From where the sinew held the ends together, she tied an additional, very thick and very strong, length of sinew. She prepared the other strap of leather in the same manner for Mary's other arm. With great gentleness and utmost respect, the woman helped Mary to her feet and led her to a place in the back of the cave that had overhead beams supporting the ceiling.

Mary by now knew that she was in the care of a wonderfully talented woman. The woman instructed Mary how she was to suspend her weight from the leather straps with her arms, and to grip the top of each leather loop with her fist. Then the woman tied each loop to a beam and helped Mary to slip her arms through the loops, thereby allowing Mary to relax her lower body. Gravity would be her friend. Her baby would come easily. Women had been delivering babies for years using this skill.

Mary was not ashamed of her nakedness before the woman. Was not the human body the purest form of innocence before God's eyes? The woman's fingers found Mary's back, and with more gentleness than what Mary thought was possible, she massaged Mary's shoulders and back and hips with the freshest of oils. The woman, now absorbed in her task fully, sang the tenderest of lullabies to Mary and the baby. It was only then that Mary knew she could fulfill her task.

From her heart, Mary prayed as she had not prayed before. Only the nearby animals heard her pleas for strength and her cries of pain. The woman did what she could to reduce Mary's pains, including placing a length of leather into Mary's mouth for her to bite on. As if on cue, all of the animals stopped chewing their cuds and swishing their tails for a slow moment in time. Silence reigned.

Joseph had run out of prayers and firewood. He dared not converse with the other families because he wanted his ears to listen to the cave. He was trying to make himself busy by analyzing a tree stump for what lumber it would yield when he heard a tiny, thin wail from within. His feet froze to the dirt, wanting to rush in. He heard the pulse pounding in his ears. Now he paced aimlessly, not realizing that men had done this thing for centuries before him, and would continue it for many centuries after.

"Joseph." The call came softly, but he heard it over the commotion of the other families. He quickly picked up the jar of warm water and hurried inside, still not sure of what he was supposed to do. The lamp gave off a faint glow, enough to illuminate the faces of two women and a babe. Joseph looked at the woman in the corner, only to see her smile. Before he could utter his thanks, a strange thing happened. The woman dematerialized into thinness, into nothingness. Where she had stood was now a faint misty cloud. She was no more. *An angel*, Joseph thought.

Mary was sitting against the grotto wall. Her face was clean, her hair brushed, her smile radiant in the soft glow of the fire. She beamed faintly and nodded for Joseph to approach. Then with Joseph's help, she stood. They approached the manger where Jesus lay. Joseph could not see much of the baby because he was so carefully swaddled in the long, narrow strips of cloths, as was the custom of wrapping newborns to help the baby grow straight and tall. *Mary was smart*, he thought. She had brought swaddles in case she gave birth while on the trip. He was amazed at seeing his extra mantle being used as a pillow for the tiny head. In place of fodder was the Savior. A balmy glow of soft white light flooded the baby's face.

This was the Messiah. This was the Holy Spirit incarnate as the Child of Promise.

He did not look like a Messiah. He was tiny, like any other infant; he did not cry. His face was flush and his hair was still wet. He did not stand tall and issue orders or command attention. He did not roar with authority nor did the populace flock to hear him proffer leadership. He was a simple baby born a simple birth in a simple cave. His mother and father were ordinary citizens of an ordinary country. Mary had suffered the discomfort of gravidity and the pangs of labor the same as any other mother. No, he did not look like a Messiah.

Yeshua, you and I will come to know each other intimately. We will grow together and walk the miles in stride. Your coming is a blessing to all of humanity. We are one; we are friends through Spirit.

CHAPTER 10

Summer 7 BCE

~⌣⌣∧

In the Grotto

After passing the night in that miserable room, my friends and I found the census-taker and we registered ourselves to fulfill our obligation to Caesar. I bade them safe journey for their trip home. Feeling good about completing my mission, I sought out where Joseph and Mary had found refuge. With only small effort, I was able to find them in their grotto.

"Chaim, my friend, *baruch haba*, welcome! to our little place of shelter," Joseph cried when he saw me. "We did not know where you went when we separated on the road. I am glad you found us. Please, enter. Be welcome."

"Indeed, it is my pleasure to see you and Mary again." I turned to Mary. She was a picture of delight, holding the baby in her sweet arms. "Mary, bless you, child. You look radiant."

"Thank you, friend." Mary remained quiet and reverent.

"This is the baby Jesus?" I whispered as I knelt before them, saying a silent prayer for the miracle and removing the scarf from my head. "He is a beautiful baby, beautiful indeed! Praise to God for giving us the promised Messiah after so many centuries."

"He will grow quickly, I am sure of it," said Mary mildly. "He will be a strong boy and a fine man."

Joseph stood and prepared to find the census-taker. He saw to my needs before he departed to fulfill his task. "You are comfortable, Chaim?"

I smiled.

He turned to Mary. "I will return soon. I must find the census-taker to complete my obligation to Caesar. Mary, God be with you and our son." He hugged her and kissed the baby and departed. I overheard his prayers fade into the air as he walked from us.

When he was gone, Mary opened up to me. "He is a good husband, Chaim. I love him so much. He is good to me; he is a good provider."

"That I know."

She went on. "I am sure the authorities will allow Joseph to represent our new baby and me. The census-taker needs to realize the reason we traveled to here. We need and want to be law-abiding citizens of Nazareth. He will return shortly."

"Mary, tell me," I hesitated. "*ma shlomex*, how are you doing? Are you comfortable? What do you feel about the new one?"

"Even though he is a newborn, I fill my hours in bliss, Chaim. I love to sit with him and rock him. I did not sleep last night at all." Mary radiated love. "I love to coo and talk to him, as if he were an ordinary little baby. To me, he is of course, and is so much more. I adore the feeding times with him. Nursing him is an ecstatic feeling for me, knowing that I am responsible for nurturing him through his infancy and boyhood. What a big responsibility I have. I am proud of him. Only I can give him the maternal care and love that he requires."

I could only kneel in awe. I was in the presence of the Master Teacher. "How is Joseph doing?" I asked.

"He is wonderful. He knew not what to do yestereve when Yeshua was born. He was helpless, and I love him even more for that. He and I learned beautifully together our first night how to care for my needs and that of our son. He is a good man and I love him deeply. He misses working his trade. It has been a *shavua*, a week so far, and he does not want to lose favor with the townsmen who give him employment if he does not return in reasonable time. He loves his work."

"Yes, you are fortunate to have one another."

She shifted Jesus in her arms as he whimpered in his sleep. "Joseph and I talked last night. We decided that we want his circumcision ceremony to take place in Jerusalem, in the Temple of Temples. That would be eight days from now. Then, as you know, I need to present myself to a priest in a temple or a synagogue on the fortieth day after his birth for my purification ceremony. It is written in the law."

Mary spoke slower now, reflecting in her humility. "And because of the specialness of this birth, we want that ceremony to take place in Jerusalem, in the Temple of Temples as well. The excessive travel to home and then back to here would place too much anxiety on all of us. We will stay here. We know that no one will object to our staying in this little cave, and we can make it quite comfortable for our needs. It is not what we had expected when we left Nazareth; nevertheless, it is quite adequate for our humble requirements. The other pilgrims will be returning to their homes, and we will be fine here."

She studied the beams overhead for a moment and then said, "Chaim, you are our very best friend. Joseph and I have known you for our entire lives. I must ask you a question. Will you remain here in Bethlehem with us for those forty days? I mean, would staying here burden you to any excess? Will you miss your work and your friends in Nazareth? Joseph and I do not want you to feel uncomfortable in any way by staying here with us."

"It will be my privilege to stay with you for that time," I said. Thinking fast, I knew that I would be able to obtain a cheap room in the guesthouse, with all of its shortcomings, now that the swarms of pilgrims are returning to their homes. Too, I remembered the vow I made to myself to relate this chronicle for as long as possible. "By doing so, I will be able to see and feel all that happens to you and Joseph, and of course to the baby. By some faint urge that is deep inside of me, I feel compelled to be with each of you so that I may document everything that happens. I will be honored to do so."

Every time a Jewish woman gives birth, she is considered unclean for seven days afterward. Then for the following three-and-thirty days, she is to remain in "the blood of her purification." At the end of the forty days, the new mother is to bring a lamb or two turtledoves as an offering to a temple. The proper Jewish purification ceremony deems forty days to be the right amount of time for the woman to become clean again. Leviticus dictates these things to us.

I continued with my thoughts. "I am happy for you, Mary, and for your family. I am proud to know you and to see the little one so peaceful in your arms. You are a good mother; I know you are."

"Chaim, thank you for being such a good friend to Joseph. He values your friendship. He is a strong husband. You are just what he needs, especially now that we are away from our homes and in another land, even if it is our homeland. He and I are grateful for your friendship and your sage guidance. You are older; you are wiser. You are like a father to both of us."

"Mary, friend," I said, "do not praise me. I am to extol you. It is my duty to praise you and the infant. That is why I came this hour to find you. Be proud of yourself, Mary, for you have done a good deed—nay, a great deed—in birthing Jesus into the world. You have brought us the Savior we have been seeking for so many generations. May God bless you in these great hours. I know God will shower you with untold blessings."

I could see that all that had happened to her these past hours and days humbled Mary. She was, after all, a straightforward citizen of Nazareth who was merely doing what needed to be done. Given the fact that she had been visited upon by the Infinite Spirit to bear a son was indeed astounding. Given more that she had endured the months as a normal mother-to-be was also remarkable. She knew she had carried the weight of the world inside her womb.

"I return." It was Joseph. "I found the census-taker and told him my name and yours, Mary. I told him that you were with our new child and that the baby's name is Jesus of Nazareth. He made the marks on his scroll in the proper place and nodded at me. He was satisfied that I represented you so that you did not have to go there with me. I did what we came here to do, and I am pleased that I have fulfilled the law."

"Thank you, Joseph," said Mary. "I am glad you could register for me in my stead. Chaim and I have been in grateful conversation while you were away. We are thankful of the joyous juncture that has been bestowed upon us."

"Yes, Joseph, I was saying how proud I am of Mary. She has brought on the world a mighty man who will deliver all peoples of great transgressions. You should be pleased of her, my friend."

"Indeed I am."

"Before I go, may I ask of you two a question? It concerns Jesus."

"Of course."

"My long and proud Jewish heritage urges me to call the baby Jesus ben Joseph. You know that that means Jesus, son of Joseph. I cannot resist the urge to do so. I feel right about his proper Jewish name."

"Chaim, friend, you are right. I would like you to call my son Jesus ben Joseph."

"I depart. *Barchot ve Tefillot*, blessings and prayers on you."

CHAPTER 11

Summer 7 BCE

Brit Milah

It is eight days after the birth. The eighth day of life for a Jewish boy is a very important day. It is then that a sacred rite takes place. The boy is presented to the rabbi in the Temple for circumcision. The ceremony represents a sign of the covenant between God and his preferred people. It shows that my people have been chosen for a very special destiny.

The ceremony for circumcision is called Brit Milah and it means, "The Sign of the Covenant." That covenant is between God, Moses, and the Jewish nation. I quote from our Scripture. "This is my covenant which you shall keep between me and you and thy seed after you. If a woman conceive seed, and bear a man-child, then she shall be unclean seven days; as in the days of the impurity of her sickness shall she be unclean. And in the eighth day, the flesh of his foreskin shall be circumcised; every male child among you shall be circumcised." The ceremony is customary in the entirety of the civilized Jewish world.

Even on holidays like Shabbat or Yom Kippur, it is performed. It is our tradition that the ceremony be made as early in the day as possible. If the baby boy is not healthy—and Jesus ben Joseph is without a doubt healthy—then it may be delayed. Jesus is fortunate, indeed blessed, with having the ceremony performed in the Temple. Any priest may perform the Brit Milah in a synagogue, a public place, or a private home.

Apprehension

Joseph and Mary followed the prescription properly.

"Are you nervous?" Joseph asked of Mary.

"A little." She paused. "Yes, a lot. I know that today is a significant one. Our baby is taking his first step to becoming the Messiah that the prophecies predicted. Imagine, Joseph, our little Yeshua, our little boy is the *Moshiah Olam*, the Savior of all humankind. What an awesome responsibility that is! I cannot visualize how he will be when he is a man, but I know he will do well. Oh, Joseph, I wish I knew how he will proceed and how much he will suffer in his mission. There are so many things I wish I knew about him. There is so much I do not know, and as a mother, I must look out for his best wellbeing."

"Likewise," continued Joseph, "I share your consternation of Jesus. I do not have any answers as to how he will fare in his adulthood. I, too, am lost in concern for him. I am trying to be calm. I will be calm for it is important for the day to progress smoothly for Jesus. Yes, today is an important day in the life of our Jesus. Look how peacefully he sleeps."

Joseph paused to look up and all around where he stood. "Mary, my friend, are you sure you understand the meaning of today's Brit Milah?"

"I am sure; at least, I think I am sure." Mary knew inside her being what the ceremony entailed, but her nervousness confused her mind. "Love, maybe you had better explain it to me again."

"I share your disquiet. Let me explain further for you." Joseph studied his sandals and thought for a minute before he spoke. "The circumcision is a symbol of cutting off of mortal tendencies, and is indicative of purification and cleanliness. The man—in this case Jesus—is purified from the laws of sin and death. He manifests wholeness and perfection throughout his being. He is free of all mundane and worldly thoughts and activities."

"Thank you, my love, for explaining it for me. Now I can understand what will come to light today."

It was Mary's turn to contemplate in silence for a short while. Then, "The sun is filling the east. We must be prompt. People—important people—are arriving for the ceremony. We must begin. He is a pretty boy, is he not? We must not be late." The pair made their way through the Golden Gate, sometimes known as the Gate Beautiful, on the east side of the Temple. The Gate Beautiful exemplified the way for mankind to attain spiritual illumination. That gate gave access to the courtyards where most of the ordinary people conducted their daily business.

Mary paused in awe to look around in all directions, for she had not been inside the Temple before this day. She lifted Jesus out of his basket to adjust the swaddling over him, and then chose a quiet corner to sit in while she nursed him. "The day will be a blessed one, that I am sure." Wisely, she chose the corner on the left of the gate, for to the right was the Temple's treasury, and she did not want to disrupt the place of gathering and counting of the offerings. From the corner of her eye, she saw the thirteen trumpet-shaped containers inside the treasury that collected voluntary offerings of money.

Herod's Temple

I know Joseph. He is a curious man, for he is a builder like me. He cannot be in such a breathtaking edifice and not wonder how it is constructed. What a magnificent structure it is!

The First Temple, sometimes called Solomon's Temple, had been constructed nine centuries earlier by King Solomon. The Babylonians destroyed it five centuries ago. And now King Herod was building another Temple on the same hallowed grounds. Herod began its reconstruction twenty years ago by clearing and enlarging the ruins of the first temple.

Some portions of the temple were complete, while other areas, notably those on the outside, were still under construction. The stones in the walls shone in the sun's rays. Every block, every portico, every courtyard radiated a richness that was not to be found anywhere else.

Herod was sure to include in his masterpiece a magnificent water garden, an amphitheater, and a hippodrome. In keeping with the tradition that forbade Herod from building beyond the first temple's original dimensions, he added a thirty-five acre platform under the actual Temple.

Yes, this was indeed the home of the spirit, the place of the heart. So while Mary tended to Jesus, Joseph set out to explore what he could see. He was struck with its sumptuous beauty.

It seemed like all, or at least most, of Jerusalem was *hechal*, holy ground. Over the centuries, according to our Scriptures, much history happened here in this very city. Any common goat herder could see the shining Temple from a distant hilltop. Its prominence was Herod's intention. All of the arched cloisters were edged with double pillars. Each pillar was twenty-five cubits in height. Each pillar was hewn from a single white marble stone. Incomparable decorations adorned walls and ceilings everywhere. Ornamental cedar showed prominently. The inside of the Temple was more decorative than the outside. Even though the grand Temple was built by Herod the Great, the people everywhere called it their own Temple. Herod built this great Temple as a tribute to himself.

In the strictest of interpretations, no graven images were allowed to show publicly. That was why the most decorative of decorations were inside the most restricted parts of the Temple. The outsides of the Temple were less ornamental than the insides, but nevertheless were still beautiful to behold.

A graven image was a replica of a human form or face that could be used as idol worship. A graven image could also be the image of an animal or any other object that could be used for worship. Any image that could be used as a form of worship was forbidden. Our money, the shekel, has no portraits on it; it does not promote the worship of graven images.

By the same logic, the home of any ordinary Jew reserved the most attractive of objects for the inside of the house. The outside appearance of the house was plain and simple.

In the Temple, every juncture of every wall, floor, and ceiling was joined perfectly; not even a scrap of parchment could pass between them, so tight were they touching. The harmony of the polished cloisters on the outside wall made a very distinguished facade. Each of those covered walkways was thirty cubits in breadth. The entire construction measured six furlongs, including the Tower of Antonia.

Eight gates made openings into the Temple. The inside of the Temple was arranged as one area within another area. Each inner area was more sacred than the one around it. Anyone could enter the outer area and its name was called the Court of the Gentiles, for as its name implied, any non-Jew and Jew could enter into that area.

The next inner court was called the Court of the Women, the furthest quarter into which the Jewish women could go, and then only when accompanied by a man. At the far end of this court was the place where Mary and Joseph brought Jesus for his presentation.

After the Court of the Women stood a handsome stone balustrade to keep the people at their proper place. Signs, carved in Hebrew and Greek, warned the uncircumcised to enter not, upon penalty of death. To be exact, the words read, "No foreigner is to go beyond the balustrade and the plaza of the Temple zone. Whoever is caught doing so will have himself to blame for his death which will follow."

Behind the stone balustrade was the Court of the Men, the furthest place where ordinary Jewish males could go. Past that was the Court of the Priests where, in its center, the priests made their burnt sacrifices on a holy altar. To the altar's left was a large basin cupping twelve bulls cast in bronze. More steps led up to the actual Temple. It was a small building. An embroidered map of the known world concealed its entrance, and only the priest on duty was allowed to pass beyond that curtain. When the priest entered that chamber, he knew the golden altar at which he offered burnt incense greeted him. Next to the seven-branched candelabrum was the table where he offered the twelve unleavened loaves of shewbread each Sabbath.

At the far end of that room was another large curtain that divulged the Holy of Holies. Only the high priest could enter that room, and only on the Day of Atonement. A stone there marked the place where once the Ark of the Covenant stood. The Ark of the Covenant was that holy chest that held the Ten Commandments inscribed on stones tablets.

This sacred Ark of the Covenant represented the original spark of divinity in man's being. This original spark was holy because man's immortality rested with its maturation. When the Ark was removed from the heart center—the city of Jerusalem—the spiritual forces were scattered. The Ark was a covenant of the Holy Spirit with all of humanity such that every human being would inherit all that the Holy Spirit could offer. Spiritual understanding of the atonement showed the reconciliation between God and mankind.

I can divine through the grace of God that one day, this Temple will crumble to the dust of the earth by way of a man's hand. Only the *Kotel Ma'aravi*, the Western Wall of the Temple will remain. The Western Wall is that wall opposite the Gate Beautiful. The Gate Beautiful is on the eastern side of the Temple. Sometimes I fear for my sense of prophecy, as it is great and it frightens me.

The Ceremony

I saw Mary and Joseph coming this way. Mary enfolded Jesus in the cleanest swaddles she owned. "Yes, the two chairs are prepared," stated Joseph. "I will serve as the Sandek, the one who holds the baby during the ceremony. The other chair is set aside for the spirit of Elijah the Prophet, The Angel of the Covenant."

Joseph paused to take a deep breath. "Our custom is this. Elijah comes to all Brit Milahs to testify to God that we Jews are committed to this great commandment, that of keeping the covenant with God. Just before the ceremony, the boy is placed on Elijah's chair and the Mohel, the man who will perform the circumcision, recites a prayer. He beseeches Elijah to look after the baby and help the baby endure the pain. The prayer asks Elijah to help him to perform the ritual according to law.

"After the Mohel has performed the Brit Milah, he blesses a goblet of wine and asks of me the name to be assigned to the baby. I will answer, 'His name is Jesus.' That is his Hebrew name; the angels gave it to him while he was still in the womb. I can see that a Minyan is here, too. A Minyan is ten males who are to be present as witnesses; we have many more than that here, for this is a singular, glorious occasion. History will mark this ceremony well."

"Well done, husband of mine," said Mary. "As you know, it is our custom to name a boy-child after a righteous man or a departed male relative. The angel Gabriel gave us the name Jesus, and that is his name. Jesus means Yeshua in Aramaic, which means, 'Salvation.' One of our purposes in finding salvation is to learn to let go of our erroneous beliefs."

To me, he will always be Jesus ben Joseph.

CHAPTER 12

Late Summer 7 BCE

A Visit with Elizabeth and Zacharias

In the excitement of birthing her boy, Mary did not forget her cousin Elizabeth. On the day following the birth, Mary asked Joseph to arrange for a messenger to send word to Elizabeth of the news of the birth. Late the next day, the messenger, a man named Boaz, meaning, "Swiftness," returned with a message of his own. Zacharias and Elizabeth invited Mary and Joseph to come to their domicile for a visit and to see the baby to be known as John. Knowing that they were planning to wait in Bethlehem for the forty days to pass for Mary's purification ceremony, Mary and Joseph made a plan to visit Zacharias and Elizabeth in Ain-Karem, but not before Jesus' Brit Milah ceremony on the eighth day.

The day following the Brit Milah, Mary and Joseph and their baby made the short trip to visit Elizabeth and Zacharias. Mary, being young and resilient, felt little discomfort of the jostling donkey under her. Her concern was not for herself, but rather for the comfort and protection of her baby. She was extra careful to cradle and clasp her precious cargo.

They stayed three days there. Joseph and Zacharias discussed topics such as conforming to Jewish law and how the birth of the Messiah would impact the future of their faith. Mary and Elizabeth, being proud new mothers, coddled and admired both babies with great passion. The babies looked remarkably alike in features and size.

The four of them agreed, with sincere conviction, that Jesus was indeed to become the much-proclaimed Light of Life and deliverer of the Jewish people out of repression. The four of them agreed further that John was to be Jesus' primary and first disciple of destiny. Their hope was that the two young boys could grow up together, but they knew that might be difficult, as Joseph and Mary had plans to return to their home in Nazareth soon. Their time together was all too short, and the family made its way back to their temporary home in the grotto.

Order. During the return trip, Mary and Joseph for the first time noticed the deeply verdant vegetation and blossoming flowers along the sides of the road, as their minds were now at ease and could be thankful for the passing scenery. They knew that divine order was at work in their lives to give them the goodness that was theirs forever, and that only goodness could come their way. They knew they were following whatever plans God had in store for them.

Even as they knew that God had a plan for them, they knew, too, that they had a free will to do what they would do. They knew that every decision and every experience they had undergone in the past led them to be exactly where they were now, in this moment in time. Their lives proceeded in an orderly way.

Their journey was in fact a journey of consciousness development and alteration. To them, personal growth meant finding and loving God even more than they had thought possible in their lives. I had never seen such a thing before in the young people. The change in their lives was remarkable to me. I saw them transform from ordinary villagers to highly respected citizens.

Lights in the Sky

Here I must expand my story of the great event. I can be so perplexed at times due to the confusion that runs through my mind as I see this cavalcade of wonderful historic events passing before my eyes. I feel that it is time for me to go backward in time, back to the day and the hour of the birth that I have so hard tried to describe. I want to fill in some details while they are fresh in my mind.

The word Bethlehem means, in Hebrew, "House of Bread" or "Place of Food." The true meaning of Bethlehem can be felt only by being there, by smelling the smells and hearing the sounds in the lanes and in the marketplaces. I like to think that Bethlehem symbolizes the abiding place of substance, where universal matter joins spiritual ideals. In Bethlehem, love and wisdom unite to bring forth God's Spirit into manifestation.

During the night of the birth and in the skies above Bethlehem, a curious thing happened. It is something I cannot explain. I have a scholarly friend named Zohar, meaning in Hebrew, "Bright Light," who knows of the astronomy of the stars and he did explain it to me. He told me that a rare sequence of events occurred at the same time Jesus was born. I can remember what he described. The remarkable series of stellar measures was this.

Three extraordinary events happened in our heavens this very year of Jesus' birth. Three times a great light materialized in the night's firmament. My instinct tells me that firmament represents faith in the invisible. The planets of Jupiter and Saturn juxtaposed in the constellation of Pisces to produce a brilliant spot of light over the mountains of Moab in the east. Each of these significant and natural astronomic events gave a great brightness to one place in the sky. It was as if one magnificent star appeared for a few days and then dispersed as quietly as it had appeared—three times. Such a triple Jupiter-Saturn conjunction is most rare. I know what happened. I saw the bright light with my own eyes, each of the three times.

To clarify my description, I list an order here. The first conjunction appeared in Sivan, late spring, three months before Jesus' birth. Jesus was born in the month of Elul, late summer. The second conjunction appeared one month after Elul, in the month of Tishri. Finally, the third conjunction appeared three months after Jesus' birth, in the month of Kislev, early winter.

I never quite know who to believe. Shepherds tell me that the third conjunction, the one in Kislev, was the brightest of them all. They say it was brighter than a full, round moon, but not as big as the moon. The brightness cast shadows from everything on the ground. It is mysterious to me.

Three occurrences within one brief timeframe, I understand, could be basis for a great fable for future generations. In the grand plan of things, they were so close together that they would be, as memory would recall years later, one and the same. Word-of-mouth stories from one generation to the next could become a myth. From that, the story could become a tradition. Lastly, I know that the tradition could easily become established as a fact. That I know. I know the human mind; I know my people. We love to embellish the ordinary into the extraordinary. Stars that announce the Messiah's birth occur not once in a lifetime, but once in a forever. The light of all the stars represents the light of our intuition because it is always with us as it guides us in the way we need to go, step by step.

Look at the sky! Look at the winds and the rains and the rocks! Are they not tiny specks in time? Are they not simple flashes of light, blazing before us in a second, even before we can blink our eyes? When we turn around, our children have children of their own. How did that happen? When did that happen? How can God be so good to us? Does God's love ever tire of giving? Thank you, Immeasurable Spirit, for all blessings.

The Shepherds

In the valley below Bethlehem, those men watching their sheep sat on rock precipices overlooking their flocks. They faced another night of near-boredom. I cannot blame them for their tedium. Sheep are interesting animals, but to be responsible for them day after day, night after night, can bring monotony. I know they are part of God's creation, as I am, but admittedly, they are not mentally stimulating. Any excitement that comes to the men is surely a welcome diversion in their habit.

By day, their routine was different; the business of the sheep kept them fully occupied. The herds wandered freely on the grasslands. The idea was to let the sheep eat until they sated. Fat and healthy sheep are what the sheep watchers wanted. Fat and healthy sheep without blemish brought a good price as sacrificial animals in the Temple, as did the goats in similar fine condition. The less perfect animals, those sheep and goats with blemish or imperfection, were sold for shearing and for food.

Apart from the shepherds were the swineherds who stank of their burdens. From a distance, the flock looked like a sea of beige barrels floating over the grasslands. Pigs could be just as unpredictable as sheep. Even a wrinkling of the wind or the snapping of a twig could disturb them to unrest. I know this to be true. In unison, each head could sniff skyward with woofing sounds. They could snort, stiffen their tails, and begin a stampede for no reason. This behavior did not happen often, but the swineherds had to be on constant guard nevertheless.

The shepherds knew that they did not need the exact timing of the stellar conjunctions to herald Jesus' birth. They knew only that the time had arrived to proclaim the birth so very long awaited. God's hand spun the stars in the skies without ceasing. God's hand brought a newborn child to all of humanity. How could it be any more perfect?

When Jesus was born, the angels spiraled downward in every direction, radiating the purest of whiteness and filling the hills with thousands of bell-clear voices. The donkeys and mules and horses stamped the ground. The sheep bleated unceasingly. Doves and all birds flocked skyward, patterning the air with delight. Frogs croaked, snakes hissed, and owls hooted. Each animal in its own way celebrated the birth of the Savior. Even the fish in the seas splashed the surface with their tails, and leapt as best they could to see the commotion above them. This was the expression of God in the highest! Every heart beat with great joy!

CHAPTER 13

Autumn 7 BCE

The Good News

When the first planetary conjunction happened in the month of Sivan, three months before Jesus was born, the herders and husbanders working and living around Bethlehem were afraid greatly. The brilliance was indeed frightening. They, or anyone else, had never seen anything like that in the skies. They thought such an event would be the first, last, and only one of its kind in their lifetimes. It was not. They called to their animals to remain calm. It is fortunate that the animals learn to recognize their master's voice and be calmed by it.

It took them three full months to calm their flocks back to a normal way of life. That would make it Elul and that is when Jesus was born. It was not another planetary conjunction that caused them their next great uproar. It was the Angel of the Lord.

Above them, a form materialized amid a wide and brilliant glowing radiance. "Do not fear," the angel said slowly, allowing the words to fill the valley. "I bring you Good News of great joy which is to come for the whole nation."

Did the angel say good news? We Jews have been afraid of the justice and vengeance of God for centuries. We have worshiped carefully, taking care to prescribe to all of the nuances of ritual, for fear that God would be displeased and smite unhappiness upon our tribes. And now good news? How can there be good news in the darkness of the night?

Is it not true that our Scriptures castigate us repeatedly to fear God? Even the prophet in Deuteronomy tells that we "shall fear the Lord your God; you shall serve him and swear by his name." Overcoming fear is not an easy human trait. Our Scriptures tell us to fear God, yet our hearts tell us to love God. What are we to believe? How are we to behave? God gives us those answers.

Those tending flocks looked up and the angel again spoke, this time clearly and directly at the shepherds. "A Savior, who is the Messiah, Lord of Lords and Host of Hosts, was born to you this season in David's town. This will be your portent. You will find an infant, and you shall know where to find him, wrapped well in swaddles, who awaits your visitation upon him. Go. Find him. Kneel before him and worship him, for he is the Good News."

This was better than good. This was the long-awaited promise made by God a long time ago through the prophets. It was the advent. God, by way of common people, would present the Good News to humankind.

Even though I am a faithful and loyal Jew to my core, I am slow to accept this "Good News" without some hesitancy. We as a people have been waiting for this message for centuries, as the Scriptures tell us. Now, suddenly, out of the darkness of night, over the desolate hills of a minor province in a small country, comes the Light. I am glad. I am relieved. At the same time, I am slow to accept this message fully because it presents itself so suddenly and so overwhelmingly. It is good that others see the Light with me. It is good that they can understand its significance with me. Knowing Mary and Joseph helps me to accept the Good News as great news.

The early autumn air did not feel cold at all. Why should it? This was a time for rejoicing. The shepherds' eyes drifted to the rocky hillsides to absorb the full import of the angel's words. As around the angel's face, so also were the hills aglow with the effulgent light. No shepherd slept. No animal slept. This happening was real. Hundreds of angels, all emanating brilliant light more luminescent than daylight, now joined the messenger angel.

From these bands of angels now came a rapturous anthem, "Glory to God in the heavens above, and on earth peace to men of goodwill." The chorus lasted what seemed like many minutes. Their aural glow was everywhere. The light made the night seem like the day.

The Messiah had finally arrived in his fullest glory and the angels could wait no longer to announce with the greatest of delight to the world:

GLORY TO GOD IN THE HIGHEST!
AND ON EARTH, PEACE TO ALL!

As if by magic and on cue, like a flock of birds turning as one, the angels thinned slowly into nothingness, a mere mist, and vanished into the very air. They had delivered their message.

The older shepherds were sure this was not a fraud on their eyes. All Jews were good students of the Scriptures. God had promised a Savior who would come through the House of David—Bethlehem, right above them, right up that rock-strewn path a few miles. They knew this was not the trick of an evil Egyptian magician who wanted to steal their flocks.

The Shepherds' Gift

What baffled the elder shepherds was that they could not imagine the Messiah being born in the poor village of Bethlehem. He was supposed to arrive on a great white cloud, surrounded by trumpeters flourishing heavenly music and wearing regal robes. What happened to the magnificent white horses drawing gold-clad carriages bearing harpists and messenger angels?

The shepherds, after recovering from the brightness of the lights and the euphoric feelings that flooded over them, knew they had to do something special for the Savior. They immediately went to their tents and, with their wives' guidance, prepared a gift for the baby. In only a few days' time, they had prepared their gift. They slept little each night because they wanted this special gift to be the best they could make it. They went so far as to wash their garments in the brook. They brushed their hair and scraped the dung from their sandals.

Leaving a few of their own shepherds to guard the flocks, as was the custom, the shepherds set out to climb the hills to Bethlehem. After their travel, they reached the edge of Bethlehem, where they began to mingle with the ordinary citizens, those begging on the streets and those carrying out their daily commerce. No one seemed to know exactly where the baby was. Most had heard of a recent birth; some had not. Some did not care in the least. Some town citizens were downright rude to the shepherds because they were not welcome in the village. How dare they beleaguer everyone they met on the street just so they could seek out an infant? Did they not have any manners? Had they taken too much grape?

Ordinary shepherds were not welcome in the towns because they were, after all, common vagrants, without home or roots. They wore rags for clothes and smelled like the animals they chased. Their beards were ragged and they spoke in crude Aramaic, their native tongue, and broken Greek, the language of those in commerce. Did they ever bathe?

The shepherds were used to this type of disparagement. They knew that no matter where they went and what they said, they would always be outcasts of society. They knew, however, that their flock would command a high price when it came time to celebrate any holiday that called for the sacrifice of a sheep at the altar. With that knowledge, they proceeded.

Even though this band of shepherds had taken special measures to present themselves proudly to the Messiah, to the villagers this small group of shepherds appeared the same as any other group of shepherds; their efforts at hygiene had apparently failed. The villagers' snubbing did not deter them in their mission.

At last, the shepherds wandered across the steep hill that held the grotto. "Is the newborn baby here? Are we in the right place?" The shepherds, four in number, looked bewildered. "Can this be the new Messiah we have heard so much about?"

Mary looked up, only partly surprised at the intrusion. She had just changed Jesus' wet-cloth and laid him into the manger for a nap. She was accustomed by now at the almost endless stream of curious citizens impending to see the baby. "Yes, yes, this is Yeshua. Be not shy. Come in. Come in. You are most welcome to see him."

They hesitated. The one who seemed to be the elder of them, named Ronen, meaning, "Song," stepped forward first. "We stand in awe at the sight of this baby. Merely being in his presence is an enthrallment." They removed the scarves from their heads and knelt before the sleeping son, as I had done the first time I saw Jesus ben Joseph.

"Do not be afraid. He is a little baby, an infant," reminded Mary. "He cannot hurt you." She pulled back the swaddle from his face. "See, he is innocent and pure."

"We saw the bright light in the sky and we were awestruck by the angels. We came as promptly as we could come. The angel said the baby would be the Good News. We know that is true," said Ronen solemnly.

"I too saw the light," answered Mary. "It was pure light, was it not? It dazzled my eyes, and Joseph's too."

Joseph emerged from the depth of the cave. "Welcome, friends, to our humble and temporary home. All are welcome here. You have seen Jesus, sleeping now?"

"Yes, we have," said Ronen. "We have no gifts to offer other than this small package." Turning to the man beside him, "Give it to me. It is time to offer our gift."

The second shepherd, named Roi, meaning, "My Shepherd," pulled from his mantle a small bundle, wrapped neatly in a fresh goatskin and tied with a worn pink ribbon. "It is not much," he offered. "It is a simple block of goat's cheese. We—that is, we and our wives—made it for you, just days ago, when we heard the angel speak to us. It is a special recipe, handed down from our ancestors. In it are rare spices and mixed dates, figs, pomegranates, and almonds. You will find it to be a tasty foodstuff. It is all we have to offer to you."

As if rehearsed, the four shepherds each held a corner of the package and, bowing, surrendered it into Joseph's hands. "May God bless you and Mary and the baby Jesus. We are your servants."

With those words, the four men bowed again, and then turned and strode reverently into the sunlight.

Love. Joseph turned to Mary. "Blessings unto them. They are truly a radiating center of God's love, each one of them." The pink ribbon on Jesus' gift reminded Mary that indeed anyone could radiate love at any time and in any place, and that the shepherds, here and now, exuded as much love as anyone could ever exude. Love is a harmonizing force. When love shows itself, it restores man and his world to a higher level of consciousness. That is what the shepherds did for the babe.

The shepherds emanated so much love, in fact, that Joseph and Mary, and Jesus, too, could not help but notice a special glow surrounding their faces. Was it a pink glow, however faint? Were the men blushing in love? I could not help but notice that they were—ach!—blushing. They were not afraid to display their true feelings toward the baby Jesus.

CHAPTER 14

Late Autumn 7 BCE

∿⌣⌣⌢

Mary's Secret

By now, Mary and her family were fully ensconced in the cave and were following a routine schedule while waiting for the forty days to pass. Because the old woman, long since memory, had not returned to the cave, there had been no one to chase them away. No other shepherds, goat-minders, or farmers had laid claim to the comfortable cave. As if a magical hand had guided them, a band of common animal tenders came to the cave daily to feed and groom the animals, and then departed. They said not a word. Silently on their exit, they left a small package of food and water behind for Mary and Joseph. Were they angels, like the old woman? Mary knew they were gifts from God.

One morning when she was alone with Jesus, Mary had an idea that would not leave her mind. *Yeshi, my precious, a thought has entered my mind and I cannot let it go. My mind is telling me of something I must do. I must clip a small curl of your hair and keep it with me always. It will be a way of remembering you at this fresh time of your life. If I ever need to reassure myself from an uncomfortable circumstance, touching your curl of hair will calm me greatly.*

Carefully, most carefully, she found the sharpened stone that Joseph had placed in his bundle to be used as the need arose. She removed it from its cloth wrap and polished it with a clean cloth. Then, as soon as Jesus awoke from his nap, she spoke to him. "Yeshi, be not afraid as I cut a small curl of your hair. I want you to see me do this, even though you may not remember my doing it. It is important for me to carry the curl with me always. This hair I am to cut represents the growth and maturity you will undertake as you become a man. I will tell no one of our secret."

Saying a prayer to bring health and safety to her baby, she cut the curl free from his head. She decided to wrap the curl in a clean scrap of cloth and keep the precious package with her always.

Waiting

For the parents, the time of waiting for the purification ceremony was productive. More than half of that time had passed already. The circumcision ceremony and the ensuing excursion to see Elizabeth and Zacharias had seen to that. Filling the rest of the time was not a concern for Mary, for she was a busy new mother. Washing the wet-cloths, nursing, and cleaning the cave were enough tasks to keep her busy. And of course the visitors kept coming.

Nor was waiting difficult for Joseph. Being the apt artisan that he was, he did not waste any idle time. He went among the local townsmen to inquire of work. Indeed, he did find any number of assorted jobs. "*Selach li*, excuse me, I am Joseph of Nazareth and I am a carpenter. Do you have any labor to be done? I do fine work; I can build almost anything of wood."

After inquiring of several shop owners, one showed an interest. "Yes, yes I have a task for you," answered Tomer, whose meaning is, "Palm Tree." He said, "I am the owner of this leather goods shop and I make sandals and strops and other leather goods, and I need a new workbench crafted. Can you help me?"

"Of course I can. And I will."

"Good. There." He pointed to a corner. "I have saved some lumbers from my trips around the village of late. They are good lumbers and they will make a fine workbench. You look like the kind of man who can build one for me. I cannot pay you much, no more than a few shekels. But if you need work like you say you do, then you will not mind the recompense. I can share my meals with you while you are here. Take some home to your wife. The tools I have you can use for your job."

The Purification Ceremony

The autumn air began to turn chill in Heshvan. Forty days had passed, and it was time for Joseph and Mary to fulfill the law.

According to Leviticus, the mother was required to pass a ritualistic forty days of cleansing and purification after birthing a male child, and eighty days of cleansing and purification after birthing a female child. It was customary to perform this ceremony to allow the mother's physical body to heal. During this period, she was to touch no hallowed thing, nor enter into any sacred place until the days of her refinement be fulfilled. The law demanded it.

The law required that the mother bring a yearling lamb for a burnt offering, and a young pigeon or a turtledove for a sin offering unto the priest. The priest offered them before God at the altar, and made atonement for the uncleanness of childbirth; and the woman was cleansed from the fountain of her blood.

Leviticus continued. And if her means sufficed not for a lamb, then she was to take two turtledoves, or two young pigeons. The first pigeon was for the burnt offering that was a symbol for Mary's thanks to God for her many blessings. The second one represented God's forgiveness to Mary for any sin she may have committed during the forty-day waiting period. At the ceremony, the priest made atonement for the mother, by way of sacrificing the animal, and she was clean once more.

The day before the ceremony was to take place, Joseph and Mary and of course Jesus made journey to Jerusalem. Being so close to the main Temple presented every opportunity to take advantage of it. They wanted to have the ceremony occur within the Temple of Temples, inside God's greatest gift to the Jewish people.

On the morning of the ceremony, they selected a pair of young pigeons from a youthful-looking animal hawker at the gate of the Temple. They made sure to follow the instruction of Leviticus. Even though they followed all instructions of the law, it did not mean that it was pleasant. A strong stench emanated from each animal cage. Dried filth and countless feathers littered the corridor. A dealer of doves further down the passageway yelled, "Buy your sacrifice from me!" and twirled a squawking bird around in a circle with his fist. That was in the area that sold birds. Any animal sold at the gate of the Temple had its own separate area, and each area had its own particular stench and noise. Everywhere in the air was the smell of burning flesh.

During the ceremony, after the priest had said his words that needed to be said, he came to the part where he was to cut the throat of the young birds. From my vantage point where I stood, I saw Mary cringe, indeed shudder, when the priest picked up the first pigeon and held it in his hand. The knife was poised in his other hand. I could almost hear the words in Mary's mind.

Old man, old priest, even though I respect you for being here for me and being the priest to conduct this ceremony, my feelings are sad. I see the whiteness of your robes covered with much blood from many sacrifices like this one. I see dried blood hiding in your slovenly beard. Look at your sandals. Do you see the blood drippings on them that I see?

Of course I have seen blood before. Of course I have cut into a chicken or a fish for the purpose of preparing meals for Joseph and for me. Yes, the blood is there. But what you do this day, in front of my eyes at this altar, makes it difficult for me to watch with my senses. All of this ceremony is different, almost unnecessary, from preparing meals for my family.

I watched Mary squirm most uncomfortably. Her thoughts continued.

Somehow the blood of this pigeon is different. Is it more precious in some way than that from an ordinary sacrifice? Is it more sacred than normal blood? Am I seeing the blood of my precious Yeshi in some impossible way? Am I seeing a vision? Is he to be persecuted in some way that I cannot define? Will he suffer? Will he pain? Will he cry out words of despair? I grieve for his comfort.

To my mind came a faint memory of a haunting vision. Was it the memory of that disturbing dream that came to me not so long ago in my sweat-filled sleep? Was Mary seeing the same dream that I saw?

Yeshi, sleep peacefully now in my arms. Forgive me for the tears that fall from my face unto yours.

To all outward appearances, the ceremony followed fittingly and in good time. Mary was clean again, and she felt refreshed. But privately, she felt saddened at having thought her thoughts.

Mary felt worthy about what she had just done. Like all other new mothers, she had obeyed the laws and had fulfilled all of her obligations. She felt the burden of the law lifted from her shoulders.

"Joseph," Mary said quietly. "I need have a quiet time to myself. I will sit here in this discreet corner of the Temple and nurse Yeshi. You and Chaim go and do what you need to do together. I will meet you presently."

Gently, she sat against a wall and made herself and Jesus comfortable. Then she wiped her face clean with the sleeve of her mantle, hoping to erase all traces of her tears. She closed her eyes and breathed in a deep breath. She knew that she was breathing in a breath directly from God because she knew that God was the Breath behind each breath. She knew that God's presence was everywhere, in every place, always. She felt refreshed as the air expanded her lungs, filling her with light and love from the Source. She simply rested with that thought.

She recognized, too, that exhaling the breath symbolized the letting go of all of her stress of the morning. Relax and release was what she did. Simply rest, simply be. She was one with the One.

Simeon and Anna

While in the Temple, many wondrous things happened to Joseph and Mary. My friend Malachi, meaning, "My Messenger," told me of these events. Here is what he said. He simply confirmed what I had seen with my own eyes and had heard with my own ears.

There was at the time a holy man living in Jerusalem whose name was Simeon of Judea. He spent much time in the Temple, praying and praising God. Because of Simeon's holiness, God promised to grant him enough years to see the Messiah, the Savior of his people. Inspired by the Holy Spirit and in spirit, he had gone up to the Temple that day to pray. Seeing Mary and Joseph as they were presenting the child Jesus to the Lord, he knew his prayer had been answered. Walking over to them, he took the child in his arms and praised God with the words, "Now, Lord, you may dismiss your servant in peace according to your word, for my eyes have seen your salvation, which you have prepared in the sight of all peoples, a light of revelation to the Gentiles and the glory of *am yisrael*, your people of Israel."

Both Mary and Joseph were amazed at the words of the holy man. He then blessed them and said to Mary, "Behold, this child, the Light of Life, is destined for the rise and the fall of many in Israel, and a sign that will be contradicted. Your own soul a sword will pierce that the thoughts of many will be revealed."

In the Temple at the same time was an elderly prophetess, a widow named Anna of Galilee, the daughter of Phanuel of the tribe of Aser. She was of great age, having lived with her husband for many years, then as a widow until she was eighty-four. In fact, she never left the Temple, but worshiped night and day, praying and fasting. Arriving at that very time, she witnessed what was happening. Immediately, she broke out in prophecy and thanked God for the coming of the child. Wandering about the Temple precincts, she spoke about the child to all who were awaiting the redemption of Jerusalem.

Simeon and Anna were simply friends, and kept each other company in their old ages. Both were associates of Zacharias. Both longed for the coming of the Messiah, and their confidence in Zacharias led them to believe that Jesus was the expected deliverer of the Jewish people.

Return to Nazareth

When the parents had fulfilled all the instructions of the law, they returned to their home in Nazareth. By way of preparation, Joseph said, "Let us return to our home and our friends so that we can resume a normal life."

"Joseph!" scolded Mary in a friendly tone. "You know we will never have a normal life because of the magnitude of Yeshi. We will never go back to the way we were. A baby in the home changes everything. Have not you noticed, my man? Think of the past on how many people who have been blessed with a new baby. Do they not have a new life overnight, the instant the baby is born? Think of the tasks I was required to do in this grotto to care for him. Life will not return to normal, as we know it. Is your mind busy thinking of the tasks you need to resume upon our return? Do not answer that. I know you are thinking of the future of our family."

"Yes, Mary, you are right." Joseph tightened the straps around the donkey's haunches to secure the bundles for the trip home. "It is true that I am thinking of the carpentry jobs I need to resume. I had to abandon many of my clients to make the trip south. Of course, many of them had also to make the trip south; maybe I may not have lost as much business as otherwise might have been the case. I know that all prospects are not vanished."

"You lost only a few days of work and a few shekels in recompense, love." Mary cooed kisses over the baby's face. "God will provide to us whatever we need. Look at what God has given to us. A new baby—a Savior and a Messiah, no less. What could be more wonderful? Does God not provide to us food every day? Does God not give us clothing to wear? Does God not show us the way?" She stroked the donkey's head and back in a massage, knowing that the donkey, too, was a part of God's blessing upon them.

God's grace has no boundaries. God is only love. God is in everything I see.

The family returned to Nazareth where they took up residence and tried to lead a normal life.

CHAPTER 15

Late Autumn 7 BCE

∿〰〰∿

Herod's Lands

King Herod is a powerful man. He wields his authority with strong arms and hands by way of his burly bands of soldiers. It is not beyond him to execute any man or woman who crosses him the wrong way; he kills at random and without contrition. He represents the ego's power to rule over the mind; he represents the fear that would result if the ego were to lose that power. Herod blocks the idea that we can trust the God-power to lead us each day.

His personal life is not pleasant. His wine consumption knows no limit. He is half-Jewish and therefore only half-trusts us Jews. He married ten times.

He began his career as a general in the Roman army. After losing a war against the Parthians, he fled to Rome where he persuaded Caesar Augustus to restore him to power. The Roman Senate elected him as "King of the Jews" and gave him soldiers to seize the Jewish throne. He formulated his own domestic policies. Herod tried to respect the pious feeling of his subjects, that is to say, us Jews. We were not content with his rule. He drifted between allegiance to Rome and rule over us.

Herod's territory lies entirely within the Roman Empire; the Roman Empire touches every land with shores on the great Mediterranean Sea. Slaves are half of his population. From the north to the south, his land is divided into four territories that blend one into the next. They are, in the north, Galilee where my Nazareth resides; in the middle, Samaria; in the south, Judea where Jerusalem resides. His least known territory and still farther south of Judea is Idumea. West of all of these places is a large water called the Mare Internum, or the Mediterranean Sea.

South of Idumea is the Sinai Peninsula. And beyond that lies those boundless and unchartered lands of Egypt. Describing Egypt is difficult because of the personal feelings I attach to that distant land. Symbolically to me, it is a country dark in spirit because it confined my people in bondage for many years. It is possible that the dark feelings of Egypt exist in the awareness of many men, yet those feelings of darkness within do not have to remain there. All we need do is to awake to the Light of Truth and follow that Light. Knowing and trusting the Light of God is a way of overpowering the feelings of darkness.

The River Jordan defines the eastern border of the King's land. The river runs especially close to a north-to-south direction. Springs and brooks and indeed that beautiful Lake Merom feed the Sea of Galilee, which is in the north. After leaving the Sea of Galilee, the river flows south into the Salt Sea some seventy miles downriver. The lush Jordan Valley is the result.

My only travels outside of Galilee are to Jerusalem. Other than that, I know only what others tell to me. How do I know the true scope of the civilized lands? Of the Roman Empire? Where is Rome? I know best what I can see every day, and I cannot see Rome.

Herod's Dream

Coveting power is what any king does. King Herod is no exception. He calls himself, "The Great One." Under no circumstance does he want to abdicate any of it, especially to a newborn infant. How absurd that would be! He had required of himself to remain the sole ruler over his lands.

King Herod was disturbed one night by a dream. Angels came to him and whispered in his ear as he slept, "Herod, awake your senses. From Bethlehem of Judea shall come a ruler who is to shepherd my people in Israel. The new potentate shall be as a newborn babe, born under the star in the east. He shall be the new king over all the lands. It has been written by the prophets."

He awoke with a startle. What was that dream? What did it mean? Was he to surrender his power to an intruder, a baby of all things? Was he to give up all he had worked for and retreat from public life? Never! He did not know what to think. To solve this dilemma, he issued word for all of his learned scribes and chief priests to convene in his palace in Jerusalem. "What is the meaning of this dream, learned scribes and priests? What is this babe? What is this star? Tell me of its significance."

"King Herod," replied the chief scribe, "we tell you this. From within our sources of knowledgeable men, we know that there was a birth of a very special boy. The boy will grow up to become an educated and powerful leader of the Jewish tribes. Every Jewish sect in every land will welcome his birth. He will be well-versed in all sides of society, and he will give to the people a Saviorship for which they have been searching and waiting for many years. His purpose is well-defined and his lifetime will be short and concise. This we know to be true."

Herod, not satisfied with the answer of his most trusted and educated leaders, for he did not hear the words he wanted to hear, summoned the magi to his palace. The magi were those enlightened souls who held profound and extraordinary religious knowledge and advanced spiritual insights. They resided in the land of Persia and surrounding countries. Herod applied great secrecy in calling them, so as not to cause offense to his surround of educated scribes under his rule. Being a sly leader, he needed the scribes to remain loyal to him in the case he needed their services in the future. His purpose in summoning the magi was to ascertain the circumstances surrounding the holy birth. He needed to take control of this most unusual circumstance, and to do it without delay.

"Where is this Messiah?" he demanded of them upon their arrival. "Where is this boy? Learn all you can of him and come to me with a full account. Spread forth over all my lands and find him and testify to me his whereabouts. I need to know all I can know about him and his parents. When you have found him, bring me word that I, too, may go and pay him homage. Although I have the curiosity to see him, I will not tolerate him if he promises to take away my authority over my lands and my peoples."

"There was a series of stars in the sky some days ago," the wisest of the magi explained. "I saw their brightness. You saw them, too, I am sure. A display of that magnitude surely has significant import. We cannot let this event pass without investigating it thoroughly. I feel that the brightness in the sky is relevant to the birth of this mysterious boy. We depart upon your service."

The magi, through their sensitivity, knew that it was Herod's deepest intention to kill the baby by any means possible. It would give Herod the most satisfaction if he could ensure the deed by his own bloody hands. The magi felt it was their duty to investigate the mysterious birth in all of the nearby lands. To satisfy themselves of their own curiosity and to give Herod a full and honest answer to his question, they traveled throughout Judea and nearby lands. They inquired of the babe's birth in every village and of every person they passed on the roads. According to Herod's request, they did diligent work.

Days passed, and they passed slowly. Herod, I am told, grew impatient. Alas, even a king must wait for news to reach his ears.

Finally, after days of travel, the magi arrived in Bethlehem. Upon their arrival there, they asked the villagers if they knew of the holy birth.

The villagers in Bethlehem told the seekers what had happened. "It is true, oh wise ones, that the holy birth took place in our village many days before now. You are days delayed."

The leader of the magi explained, "We saw his star at its rising and have come with gifts to do him deference. We know the star has significance and we want to honor that significance by recompensing respect to the boy. Our astronomers, in concurrence with our prophets, tell us that this bright star is to coincide with the great birth."

"We offer blessings to you and your travels," the villagers said. "The family completed their obligations to the law, and then they returned to their home in Nazareth."

Disappointed but not discouraged, the magi continued their travel, this time north to Nazareth. Joy filled them at seeing the village emerge before their journey-weary eyes. Upon entering the humble home of Mary and Joseph, they saw the child with Mary. Falling to their knees, they offered him deference. They opened their robes and presented him gifts.

The Magi

It is here that I feel obliged to describe in detail the magi. After seeing them when they dignified Joseph and Mary's home in Nazareth, I felt an instant tranquility flow through me. I was at peace in their presence.

As a group, they represented the astute thoughts that are within each of us—those wise thoughts that align us with the wise ideas of intuition. Their number was seven. Seven is the number that represents fullness in the world of experience. Seven refers to the divine law of perfection for the divine-like man. The number seven is the most sacred number to us Hebrews and the most commonly used number in our Scriptures. Did not God create the earth in seven days?

Each magus was revered as possessing mystical qualities and far-reaching influence. Their authority was as much symbolic as it was sensible because of their lineage to the lordly classes and monarchies. Different magi possessed different skills. Some kept curiosity in time keeping, calendars, tides, medicine, religious mysteries, alchemy, or poetry. Others knew of philosophy, history, magic, astrology, prophecy, or science. Each magus was different. Each of them had a keen interest in studying the night skies; indeed, knowledge of the skies was essential.

Balthasar and Hor were middle-aged and were from Asia, and thus revealed olive-colored faces and black beards. These two magi wore colorful robes of silk with matching capes of fur. Their slippers were of fine leathers.

Gaspar and Yazdegerd were from established European countries and had pale skins and blond beards. They presented themselves dressed in full luxurious robes, covered by tapestries and likewise capes of fur. They wore knee breeches and silver-buckled shoes.

Melchoir and Karsudan, with dark skins and no beards, were from the vast African continent. They wore robes patterned in subdued greens and blues, trimmed in fringed gold borders. They wore intricate tortoise shell necklaces. Their sandals were weaves of cheetah and panther skins.

Magus number seven was a woman and her name was Ardnon, which means, "Blessed." Her skin was of copper and her features were fine and delicate against an aura of jet black hair. Her robes and scarves were pure white and were thrown over her shoulder imposingly. Her sandals were as of snow. She was perhaps the most influential of the group. She was the oldest of them all, both in age and in wisdom. Her strength grew from her extensive travels over foreign and domestic lands. Her home was in the highlands of Ethiopia. Growing up there, she learned patience, integrity, and respect for all things living. As a young woman, she left her impoverished home to join traveling caravans. Her travels carried her to Greece and Rome, to European cities, to Byzantium, and to the open lands of Asia. It is with this vast store of knowledge that she served as leader of the magi.

The magi did grace the infant with gifts. From inside their robes they produced gifts of superior significance. Joseph stood in awe as each of the magi presented their gift to the Messiah. Joseph, as his earthly father, accepted each gift with much reverence and humbleness.

"Blessed Jesus and Divine Counselor, I present you with this gold ingot that has been molded to resemble a crown, to be worn symbolically on your head," said Balthasar, knowing it denoted the opportunity to give wholeheartedly of himself. "It represents everything of value a man needs in order to progress on his spiritual journey." The gold likely came from Egypt, Arabia, or Persia. It symbolized Jesus' kingship on earth and the virtues the infant possessed.

Next came Hor. "This is an intricate silk brocade, infused with gold and silver threads, that is woven into a complex image of sheep tended by a haloed shepherd. I know that you, Jesus, are the Lamb of God, the pure life and substance of Being."

Gaspar revealed a lavish alabaster dish. He lifted off the top to reveal precious frankincense. "This is a gum resin obtained from various Arabian trees and is used to formulate perfumes and incense. I know the incense burns a pleasant white smoke and all priests use it in their temples. The smoke represents the prayers going to heaven. Frankincense is a symbol of your coming priesthood and the powerful prayers you will offer to the world in the form of devotion and sacredness."

Yazdegerd in his turn brought to Jesus a potpourri of spices held in a box carved of fragrant sandalwood. "These spices embody the total submersion of Jesus," looking at Joseph, "into the work he is about to perform. The fragrance is most pleasing."

Melichoir brought myrrh held in a delicate stoppered cup. "This myrrh is precious. It came from Arabia and ordinary people use it as an oil for anointing ceremonies, as incense and perfume, and as an embalming oil. Myrrh can be used to treat pain, worms, colds, indigestion, and headaches, and as a tooth cleaner. Giving myrrh represents the giving of all your tribulations to God." He paused before saying more. "The oil, when used as an embalming fluid, represents suffering; it is a symbol of death. For that I ask for forgiveness."

Karsudan, the next to present a gift to Jesus, unwrapped from a delicate silk sack a silver chalice. "For symbolism I cannot explain, yet I know."

The last to present a gift to the infant was Ardnon. "Jesus, your life is a wonderful gift from God. For that, we give thanks." From under her robes, she produced a bejeweled box. When she raised the lid to show Jesus its content, a burst of warm red rays blossomed into the room. It was a large red ruby, one of the rarest and most valuable of all gemstones. All in the room knew the redness of it represented life, love, vitality, and power. We witnessed its energy-giving warmth to every heart. I heard Mary weeping in joy. The red ruby, symbolizing life, burned its brilliance unceasingly, much like the stars had glowed so brilliantly those few evenings ago.

Life. I was so inspired by the giving of gifts to Jesus that I feel the need to relay these thoughts before they pass from my mind. Life is a gift from God. From within that gift comes the stream of consciousness that each of us possess. Life requires the directive authority of God to make manifest what we are to experience, as we know that each phase of life has its divine purpose. Giving to others what we value and what feels holy to us imparts to each of us the divinity that exemplifies life. Giving away such valuables allows us to give up those parts of us that make us feel unholy and unworthy, and returns to us a sense of cleanliness and refreshment.

People are not always aware of their duty to develop their awareness of the God-consciousness within them. In developing that awareness of spiritual gifts, men and women find that they are more than strong—they are the strength. They are more than wise—they are the wisdom. They are more than loving and orderly—they are the love and the order. They are not merely living—they are life.

CHAPTER 16

Early 6 BCE

Herod Is Shunned

Having been warned in a dream not to return to Herod and face his wrath, the seven magi went back to their countries by another route. Leaving Nazareth they proceeded west to the shores of the Mediterranean Sea and once there, proceeded along its shores southward. A long trip, it took them into the province of Idumea, which is well south of Jerusalem. Upon reaching the prosperous coastal city of Gaza, they took their well-deserved rest. Then they crossed the mountains of Idumea going east and came unto the fortress of Masada. It is from there that they crossed the Salt Sea, taking time to bathe in its therapeutic mud. Finally, they continued northward to their homelands in and around Persia.

When Herod realized he had been deceived and shunned by the magi, he became greatly enraged. To sustain his self-esteem and to exercise his power, he ordered the immediate massacre of all boys in Bethlehem who were two years of age and younger, calculating the time from the star's first appearance to the magi. Thus was fulfilled the prophecy spoken by Jeremiah: "A voice was heard in Ramah, sobbing and loud lamentation; Rachel weeping for her children, and she would not be consoled, because they were no more."

Slaughter in Bethlehem

This is the part of my chronicle where I shudder to my core when I recall the event that occurred in Bethlehem. I cannot avoid telling it. If I do not say it aloud, then I fear I may forever carry that unsaid burden on my heart until my grave. Releasing the words into the air is like seeing an eagle soar into the sky unbound and free.

The thought never occurred to Herod that abundant time had passed to allow the holy family to travel freely from one village to another. The time required to summon his learned scribes and chief priests, and then the magi to his palace, in secret no less, and to dispatch them on their mission, took many months. He realized now and altogether too late that in two years, a family could travel long distances, even traverse his kingdom many times if they so chose. What contributed to his error in timekeeping was that perhaps he misjudged the lapse in time between the birth of the boy and the magi's betrayal of him. Worse still, he did not know the whereabouts of the baby boy. Could the baby still be concealed in Bethlehem? Somewhere in Jerusalem? Was his decree to kill the baby boys all in vain?

In order to appease his desire for power and to not look weak in his subjects' eyes, Herod ordered his soldiers to do his killing only in Bethlehem. The killing had to take place. If he failed in that matter, at least he had tried and he retained his brutal reputation undamaged. If he spread his wrath any more widespread than Bethlehem, he would risk the peoples' rising up in rebellion against him for such reckless widespread murder.

Ach! What I am to say now is the gruesome part of Jesus' childhood. My friend Uri, the one who lives near Ain-Karem where Elizabeth lives, told me of many things that go on there, and I thank him for his words. Ain-Karem is very near to both Jerusalem and Bethlehem.

Herod's men showed no mercy when they surprised the village with a predawn raid. They galloped in on noisy horseback, yelling and swinging machetes and bolos in the air violently. Screaming even louder, they dismounted and broke doors without discretion. Intent on their mission, they kicked aside anyone sleeping on mats on the floor and burst into the sleeping rooms. Anywhere they found a baby boy is where they—

I cannot use the words that are on my tongue-tip. My heart is heavy with unsaid words.

In the end, the soldiers showed no remorse. When they mounted their horses and rode away, a score of dead babies littered the sleeping rooms and streets of Bethlehem. Many of the adults suffered serious injuries defending against the assassins. Any infant who appeared to be two years of age or younger was their victim. Many baby girls died in the carnage by accident.

Flight to Alexandria

After the magi departed from Nazareth, an angel of the Lord appeared to Joseph in a dream, telling him, "Take the child and his mother, flee to Egypt, and stay there until I tell you. Herod is going to search for the child to destroy him. Herod is angry because he fears the new baby will grow up and drive him from power over the land. You must flee to fulfill a prophecy. Know, Joseph, that Egypt is the place you want to be."

Joseph was startled by the angels' admonition. He stumbled in the dark as he stood, and tried to understand what had just happened to him. Before he could discern the full meaning of the message, he lost control of his legs and fell to his mat where he received another dream, this time from a trio of angels speaking in unison. "We come to instruct you to obey what you know to be true. Obey the voices in your ear. Do not disrespect our meaning. It is for the safety of the boy. Herod is irrational and he intends to spread his wrath even more than he has already. No one knows where he will send his armies. Arise. Go. Do what needs to be done, and do it this night."

Joseph, not wanting to defy such strong messages from the seraphs, rose and took the child and his mother by night and left for Egypt. "Come, Mary, we must make haste. We must travel to a safe place south of here, more south than Jerusalem. We must go to Egypt to save Jesus' life. We must go now. It is so ordained."

"Are you sure we must endure that travel?" Mary wanted to know, rubbing sleep from her eyes, unsure of what risk was to come next. "It seems like only days ago we returned from a long trip. I want to become calm in my own home, to see Jesus play and laugh with his playmates. I want to tend my gardens and visit with my friends here in the village. I want to be in my home."

"I understand your needs, Mary, but it is indeed true. We must make haste. We must go." Joseph had decided it was best. And it was best. The angels had said so.

Joseph, my darling, you know I do not want to leave our home.

We must.

Maybe we could barter with Herod's men to stay here just a little longer.

No, it is not possible.

We could try?

No.

Joseph, be reasonable. There is a way to avoid all of that grueling travel. We can do it. We must try.

No, woman. It cannot be that way.

Men! You hold so much power! You can be so persistent!

And so can women. I know. I married one.

Men!

We leave upon the darkness of this night.

We leave. Yes, we leave our home by night.

Ani ohev otach. *I love you.*

Ani ohevet otcha. *I love you.*

News from Bethlehem

The couple made fast to my house and woke me from my sleep, and pleaded with me to accompany them. Of course I did. We fled to Alexandria, protecting the baby Jesus from harm at every step. Our duty was to keep him safe and healthy. We traveled alone through the night in order not to attract any interest upon ourselves. Our faithful donkey uttered no protest.

This moment is the only moment there is. My only function is to serve.

I journeyed with them, as any good friend would do. I wanted to be with them to learn their story and relate it as accurately as I could. Admittedly, as the truth, I traveled with them because I wanted to witness as much of Jesus' presence as I could, while I could. We were there for nearly two years in that foreign land.

In Alexandria, we sought out relatives of Joseph's family. It was in their home that we stayed and lived for that uncertain time. Mary tended to her baby and helped with the domestic chores in the home while Joseph and I sought work in our respective trades. The gifts of the

Magi allowed us to meet our daily needs. Neither Joseph nor I wanted to become dependent on those gifts to sustain us. Each of us wanted to feel productive and active in the community while we were there. This is the only period in the lives of Mary and Joseph that they felt prosperous; it is while they were there that they had enough money for daily living.

Carefully Joseph concealed those precious gifts. Joseph, as Jesus' parent, felt obliged to husband those gifts to the most advantage. He was indeed rich. He had resources to sell, one-by-one as the need arose, to meet the family's daily living expenses. By the end of the second year when Herod had died, the gifts were no more. In their place was a happy and healthy family, which to me, is far more important than material objects. He was able to save some shekels for whatever the future might require. He helped to provide my needs while we lived in Egypt. It blessed us all to have the prosperity given by the gifts to sustain us during those years in the foreign land.

While we were in Egypt, we learned from the caravans that Herod's army had swarmed Bethlehem and killed all the male infants of Jesus' age.

Hearing such news both frightened and depressed Mary. It was her very own son who had been the object of such brutality. All of that happened because Jesus had been born. It happened because Jesus had been born! She shuttered in the realization that they had escaped to safety and that Jesus was safe with them in their refuge. One day, she knew, Jesus would learn of this massacre and he, too, would have to bear on his shoulders the knowledge that he was the cause of that happening.

Wisdom. Like the brilliance of the yellow sunshine each day, I see Joseph glowing in goodness, knowing that he is fulfilling his role as provider. He uses his "inner voice" to guide all he thinks, feels, says, and does. Spiritual discernment places wisdom above the other facilities of mind. Wisdom is pure knowing; it is spiritual intuition that allows us to make right choices. And by making the right choices, we are responsible for living the consequences that result from those selections.

An incredible gift of Joseph's wisdom was being able to draw upon Spirit for guidance. He—and Mary, too—were able to grow spiritually, knowing their choices were based primarily on spiritual guidance.

CHAPTER 17

5 BCE

∿‿⌣‿∿

Mary's Growth

My observations of the family encouraged me because it was their youthful vitality that kept me inspired to tell our story. The adventure of traveling here with them was both daunting and exciting. I missed my friends at home but was able to make new ones during our stay.

During the months in Egypt, I saw Mary blossom as a young wife and mother. She was very mindful and protective of her special child, but remembering Gabriel's visit allowed her to release her fears and enjoy seeing her baby grow and become a sweet toddler. Joseph smiled as he watched her care and love for their child.

Jesus' very first memories were of Egyptian sunshine in his face. He of course did not know or even care that he was in Egypt. He did not care that his parents had to flee tumultuously through the night away from a pending infanticide. Being a toddler, he knew only that his mother cared for him every hour of every day. That was all that mattered.

In the locality we were staying in the city of Alexandria, they were happy to meet other young families with similarly aged children. It was with great satisfaction that Mary watched Jesus play with the children.

To stay busy and to further support his family, Joseph made available his woodworking skills to the community. Living near the shores of the Mediterranean Sea allowed Joseph to learn more about building and repairing boats than he had learned while living in Nazareth. One memorable repair job he did was for a merchant who lived nearby. He owned a large fishing boat that had been used so much that it required profuse refurbishing. Joseph set to the task with flair. He rebuilt and resocketed the mast. He installed new thwarts and refashioned the oarlocks and fashioned a new tiller. He discovered a way to recaulk the seams of the hull with molten tar to restore its seaworthiness. Finally, he painted the surfaces with a mixture of egg whites and linseed oil to give it a new shine. The owner was so proud of his newly repaired craft that he gave us all a private outing for our family and provided the abundant meal for the day.

3 BCE

Departure from Egypt

Joseph and his family and I stayed in Egypt until the death of King Herod. Both Mary and Joseph knew that the words spoken through the prophet Hosea must be fulfilled: "Out of Egypt I have called my son."

We did fulfill those words; I am satisfied and honored that I was a part of that fulfillment.

When King Herod died, his son Archelaus came to rule the three largest parcels of his father's reign: Idumea, Judea, and Samaria. These territories are neighbors to each other and are south of Galilee. His other son Antipas came to rule Galilee. Both were dominant. Both were tyrannical. Because he knew that Archelaus was ruling over Jerusalem—in Judea—Joseph was afraid to go back there. Joseph preferred to live under Antipas, ruler of Galilee, rather than under Archelaus, ruler of Judea. Antipas was the least dominant of the three kings. The decision was made; to Nazareth they would return.

A dream followed to reinforce Joseph's decision to return to Nazareth. In the dream, he was warned not to go to Jerusalem. His past experience with the angels was good. He trusted the angels who delivered the dreams and he trusted their advice with confidence. This angel spoke. "Arise, take the child and his mother and return to the land of Israel. Those who sought the life of the child are dead."

He did not hesitate to make the necessary plans to take his wife and son north. His obligations were to protect his family and to fulfill the prophecies, which said, "He shall be called a Nazarene." Joseph felt the safety of Nazareth calling him home.

One day soon after Joseph's dream, while in the courtyard watching Jesus play with the other boys of his own age, Mary said to the other mothers, "I have grown accustomed to living here in this fine city, and I know Joseph has too. But I know that is not what is for our family. I want to return to the City of David, Bethlehem. That is where Jesus was born."

The other mothers looked at her and said, "Mary, friend of ours, you must go to be where you must be. You cannot stay here because this is not your home. You are here only because of what happened in your land. We understand that it is now time that you return to your homeland. We have been blessed to know you and watch our children grow and play together."

Mary studied how Jesus seemed to be the prominent boy in his group of playmates. She turned again to the women, now her trusted friends, and shared with them her special secret of Jesus' true calling. "As you may have learned, Jesus is a special child in his own right. He is to be the savior of our race. He is to be the one long awaited by our people. He is to fulfill many promises handed down to us in the Scriptures."

She continued sharing her heart with the women. "Joseph told me of another dream he had only a few days ago. An angel appeared to him and told him it is time to leave here and to return to the land of Israel. The angel said that Nazareth is the place where we are to live. He and I have both had good advice from the angels, and we want to obey their words with open hearts. Joseph knows that we will travel to Nazareth and not Bethlehem, and that we do it soon. I will miss not seeing Bethlehem. It would be gratifying to see the grotto again."

The women said, "Go with God and be about your trip."

Starting out early one Sunday morning, we began our journey through a circuitous route of the western highlands. The easier, more-traveled roads through the Jordan Valley were simply too risky. Vagabonds and robbers could too easily deprive us of a happy and safe future. The babe was worthy of every precaution.

Three of Joseph's family accompanied us to Nazareth. With ample foodstuffs and water and our well-rested and trustworthy beast of burden, the trip went well. Jesus, being now about age three, thought the trip was a great adventure. With every turn in the road presenting a new escapade, how could he not have a grand time of it? His childhood enthusiasm lifted the hearts of the adults around him and made the trip seem to go faster for the entire caravan. However, he did miss his Alexandrian playmates greatly. We all assured Jesus that this was his new adventure and God would always provide new friends.

Somewhere deep in his young mind, Jesus felt he had to let go of his friends and playmates and learn to accept their rebuff in so doing.

Once arrived in Nazareth, we greeted Joseph's brother who had been living in Joseph and Mary's house while we were away. The usual salutations concluded, Joseph's brother returned to his own home on the other side of Nazareth, and Mary and Joseph resumed their lives in their former home. They agreed not to mention the specialness of Jesus to anyone, at least right now, for the sake of keeping Jesus as normal as possible for as long as possible. They knew that he would have a typical yet special boyhood right here in Nazareth.

I proceeded to my own humble house nearby with relief and great satisfaction, knowing we had succeeded in our undertaking to Egypt.

Chapter 18

3 BCE

Ilan

Jesus, do you hear me? Listen to me. I have spoken to you many times since you were born. I am your friend and obedient servant. I am here to serve you. I am here to support you. I am here to listen to you and encourage you as best I know how. I am your confidant. I listen to you without making judgments. I hear your cries of anguish as you learn to understand what your people endure every day. You can talk to me. You can trust me. You can sit upon my back and think or daydream. For now, that is your job. Revel in your boyhood. I will uphold you always.

My name is Ilan. My name means, "Tree" in Hebrew. The tree on my back can only be an omen for you. Soon enough you will learn of its significance. Soon, too soon, I fear, it will be yours to bear as your life's burden. You are strong. You are resilient. God is with you always.

Jesus, I am the donkey that Mary loves so. I carried you home from Bethlehem and then to the safety of Egypt. Now I am the donkey that Joseph trusts to carry his lumbers as he performs his daily chores. Jesus, I am obedient to you. Jesus, I love you.

I know my place in this world. I represent all animal nature to you. I allow you to do your work. I am expendable if necessary. I am a tool that helps man to express his best self. I am your servant. I am meek; I am humble.

Jesus: I hear you, Ilan. Thank you for being here for me. Thank you for caring for my parents. I trust your wisdom. I trust your strength. We are one, as friends we are.

You have no need to thank me. You have no need to concern yourself with me, a simple donkey, because I am your servant. I know you love all persons. I know you love all things. I know you do care for me as strongly as you care for each person, each animal, each tree and rock on the hills. I know your heart is big and it is full of love. Blessings to you.

Jesus: Ilan, you are a model of kindness. I see you surrounded in light. You are harmony, and harmony brings peace. Do you know that? When you display your peace, your understanding of the world brings enlightenment to all those who dwell in your circle. I want you to be with me as long as you can, my friend.

Go. Play. Learn the ways of the world. I am here for you. Love like yours can hold no grievances. God gives you good orderly direction.

The Family Expands

Age four was important because now Jesus could help his father with small tasks around the workshop. Joseph had found abundant work and in fact had two men working for him when the work was plentiful. Joseph enjoyed thoroughly building anything of wood. He had no qualm about fashioning items from leather, rope, or canvas, as long as the item was part of a larger masterpiece from his own hands. Crafting is what Joseph lived and loved to do.

Jesus divided his time between helping his father in the shop and his mother in the home. How else was he to learn so much about the common lives of common people? He honed the correct usage of his native Aramaic. Greek and Hebrew conversations came easily to the boy because of his exposure to the merchants and passengers in the caravans traversing through the area. Galilee was, after all, at the crossroads of all foreign lands.

The birth of James, Jesus' first brother, was an exciting event for Jesus. He now had a playmate and a real brother! He was thrilled at the idea of having a baby brother for a playmate.

James made Jesus very happy. Happy, too, was he when other brothers followed. Joseph came next, followed by Simon and then Judas. A sister named Miriam came between James and Joseph. It is through

Jesus' helping his mother that he learned the value of helping all others. He learned family values from two of the finest.

Jesus seemed to be a font of questions. Like a sponge, he required of himself to be filled with facts and knowledge. Joseph and Mary knew it was important to fill his cup with as much information as he could understand. On many occasions, neither Joseph nor Mary could answer Jesus' questions satisfactorily. They did their best and Jesus was patient with them.

Joseph and Mary made their home a learning paradise for the children. Any child in the village was welcome always into their home. Jews in Galilee stood strong in giving moral, religious, and intellectual training to the children.

Jewish tradition stated that the mother train the girls in domestic tasks such as gardening, cooking, and sewing. The father took the responsibility to teach the boys religious and intellectual matters. It was only right that the boys received more formal education than the girls, for they, the boys, were to be the next leaders of the community.

For example, Joseph built shallow boxes into which he put sand. These boxes served as the first tablets for Jesus to practice writing his languages. He copied characters of the Aramaic, Greek, and Hebrew words. By age five, Jesus was speaking, reading, and writing fluently in all three languages. He copied maps Joseph fingered into the sand to learn geography. Each time Jesus wrote a word or drew a picture, he destroyed it immediately so as not to leave any permanent mark of his presence. That was to become his habit in life.

He played with other boys in the village. I saw him share willingly his playthings with others his age. In the far corner of his father's workshop were extra blocks of wood and piles of wood shavings. Ach! I think Jesus had a builder's streak in him like his father, because on many occasions I observed him building and stacking those pieces of wood into every imaginable mountain possible. Maybe, I think, he was using his creative inner vision to its fullest. Such a child he was!

Imagination. I remember one day in springtime when Jesus was playing in the nearby olive grove, the same grove his father walked on the Sabbath. He came upon a bird's nest that had fallen from a tree. In the nest were three eggs of a lovely light blue color. Fortunately, the eggs were unharmed. Jesus blessed them and climbed the tree with one hand while holding the nest and eggs with the other hand. He told me later that he imagined the three eggs blooming into a trinity of light blue irises.

What we create in our minds is what we create in our lives. The divine ideas we receive through dreams and visions are what we then use to mold into the shapes we desire.

Three Blue Irises

The next time Jesus saw me after finding the bird's nest, he wanted to talk to me about it.

"Chaim, did you ever find a bird's nest fallen to the ground? With eggs in it, I mean? I found one two days ago when I was meditating in the olive grove."

"Why, yes, I believe I do remember finding one, maybe, hmm, many years in the past. I must have been exploring, just like you were."

"I felt compassion for the babies and so I climbed them back up the tree and put the nest and eggs back where it was so that the mother bird could continue her nesting."

"You are a good boy, Jesus ben Joseph."

"Well, after I came back to the ground, I had the strangest sensation all over my body. It was odd indeed. I was still in my meditative state, and so thought that my awareness had been altered by my meditation."

"Was it? What did you feel?"

Jesus hesitated to form his words. "I felt like I was a channel for something I cannot explain. I felt like some greater good flowed through me. I felt like I was being used for some greater good that simply enveloped me, all over me, to my core. Not only that, I started to feel dizzy, like I had run a race with my playmates."

"Do you feel all right now?"

"Oh yes. But then I felt like something left my body. It was strange. It felt like some force flowed from my hands to that nest, as if I was sending it warmth and light. Chiam, is that what I will feel when I begin my ministry, to drain myself every time I teach the people?"

"You felt like you were sending warmth to a bird's nest?"

"I told you it was odd. I felt so drained that I had to sit on the ground and breathe hard. I think that if someone else had been there with me, he may have seen a glow around my face that afternoon. And you know what, Chaim? I saw the three blue irises ever so clearly in my mind's eye that I reached out to pluck them from the nest itself. I was sure I would see irises in my hand."

"Tell me about this glow you sensed."

"Chaim, it was real, same as the real irises in my hand. I think the warmth leaving my hand caused a glow to spread from my hand and cover my whole body. Is that normal?"

"No, Jesus ben Joseph, it is not normal. But neither are you. You are exceptional. You know that. Accept the blush that flooded you as a taste of what you may experience when you are a man, a teacher, a rabbi. Now, go. Find your playmates and play. Be a boy. If you feel what you describe as you grow older, then you will know what it means."

1 BCE

Learning Lessons

The Sabbath forbad play on that day. At first, Jesus did not understand the concept of not playing, or working for that matter, on one day of the week. Alas, he learned soon enough, and did not fail to obey his parents when they said "No." Always, he was cheerful and good-natured.

Sabbath started on Friday at sundown and ended on Saturday at sundown. It began with abundant prayers. Mary lit the candles by which the family ate a festive feast. No one did any work; anything done was in honor of God's bounty and grace.

Mary had a sharp mind for keeping the household running smoothly. She kept on top of the animals' shelter a dovecote. With her supervision, Jesus, now age six, held the responsibility of cleaning it and keeping food available for the doves. When the family was able to sell the older squabs in the marketplace, it was Jesus who kept track of the profits. After deducting a suitable tithe for the officer of the synagogue, he donated the proceeds to a family nearby whose daughter suffered from a dreadful case of leprosy.

Likewise, Jesus held responsibility for raising the small herd of lambs they kept near their house, under Mary's supervision. Joseph told me of what happened one day while we toiled at our craft.

"Chaim, that son of mine learned a lesson yestereve."

"I know that. When he learns a lesson, he teaches you, and that is every day."

"You know of our small flock of sheep?"

"I do."

"And you know that Jesus is responsible for their wellbeing?"

"I do. It is the duty of the youngest son to watch the flock, but because his brother James is not of the age to take that responsibility, it falls naturally to Jesus."

Joseph paused to scratch his beard while he gathered his thoughts. "Yestereve, one of the frisky little lambs broke away from the main flock. It was as if the lamb had a free spirit all of its own. It just leapt around in joy, like a child playing jump the rope, and ran away. Fortunately, Jesus was there to watch the whole scene."

"That makes the lamb little different from any of us. We are all one and the same." I could tell where Joseph was leading the story.

"You know Jesus. He did not linger for one moment in time. He immediately ran after the little ball of fleece."

"He left the flock unattended?" I was not so surprised.

"Yes. Without hesitation, he ran after it. He is a good runner, as you know, and he caught up with the stray in short time. He did not hesitate to leave the main herd unattended. To him, the runaway was equally important as each one in the flock. I think he cares for every living creature equally. I know he does."

"You are right, my friend, very right," I replied. "He feels that each of us, animal and man, are equally important in spirit and in merit. God sees to that."

"Jesus showed me a new way of thinking. His heart is in the right place. I am grateful." He became very quiet for a moment, as if praying silently.

A Sprained Ankle

Mary and Joseph could not watch over the children every hour of every day. They were comfortable knowing that other women in the village watched over their family for short periods of time. Even though they knew of his special destiny, they trusted the love of the village in their children's care and trusted that none of their children would hurt themselves or become lost in the streets and alleys of the village. Naturally, the duo helped to watch other families' children whenever they could.

I mention this because on one afternoon, Jesus did indeed take a tumble. He was not injured seriously—he curled his ankle beyond its normal range of motion. The ankle swelled and turned rosy color. His knee was scraped red. I could determine that by the torturous look on Jesus' face that his wounds hurt him, and he tried not to cry. On the other hand, he could not walk on it for several days without the abet of a cane. Mary did what she could to comfort him by soaking his ankle with cool cloths and arnica bandages.

It was a simple accident, and it happened like this. Jesus was fetching the debris from the dovecote and on his way down the ladder, he slipped and fell to the ground and injured his ankle. It was purely an accident. No one took blame, and no one was assigned blame. It was part of an inquisitive and adventurous boyhood.

Jesus, I have not abandoned you. I encourage you to grow through your boyhood and then your adulthood with determination and energy, even though you will have accidents like this. You are brave. I will never leave you. I see you growing in strength and knowledge. Wisdom is yours. Great teachings come from your mouth. Even greater acts of love, healing, and devotion are yours to give to the world. You demonstrate the character of the Holy Spirit completely.

Jesus: Ilan, I see you ever around my family and me. You are a special friend. Blessings upon you.

And blessings unto you.

Jesus: Ilan, you are steadfast in your daily work. You are as solid as a stone. You help my father in his daily chores. You help my mother with her works. Peace be unto you and yours.

You stand on Holy ground. Your power is without bound.

CHAPTER 19

1 CE

Joseph's Scroll

I knew that Jesus was a smart boy. His mind was ripe and open, as a lotus in bloom. Mary, wise in her own way, taught Jesus the intricacies of the Aramaic tongue. He could converse with the merchants and ordinary folks with equal ease. As educated as Mary was, she did not speak Greek with any glibness. Here is where Joseph supplied his support to Jesus' development, for he knew Aramaic and Greek fluently, both with ease.

One of Jesus' favorite influences in the village was a rough-worn copy of the Scriptures.

"Jesus," said Joseph one morning, "this scroll was with me when I was a boy of your age. It is old even beyond that time. That is why it is worn well and smooth, and even torn on the edges. I want you to have it as your own, and to take responsibility for its use." Joseph smiled.

"I will cherish it, father. I will take pride in it, for I know that it is a source of rich heritage and history of our people." Jesus touched its texture carefully. "You can trust me with taking tenure of it."

Because there were only four other copies or partial copies of the Scriptures in the village, many people sought it out for their study and for the basis of discussion with their peers. Jesus felt privileged to meet many people streaming in and out of their home every week who sought discussions based on it. It is one way he learned of many types of personalities. I could see in Jesus' face how sincere he was when he studied the symbols on the parchment. His face illumined with pleasure at being able to understand and interpret the symbols with his adult friends.

Joseph Explains Passover

Jesus was at an age where he became curious about everything—I think he was age seven or thereabout. Joseph and I talked about his development. "That Jesus—what a boy he is!" said Joseph to me one day as we sat for our middle-of-day meal of boiled fish and a little lettuce from Mary's garden. "He has been asking me about the meaning of our holidays. He wants to know everything. And I am glad for him."

"Do you supply him with answers?" I questioned.

"Indeed I did—at least, as best as I could. I tried to be a good teacher for him. He has asked me about many of our traditions of late," Joseph said to me. "For example, yesternight he asked me what the meaning of Passover is. I did my best."

"Did you tell him in language he would understand?" I continued to probe as I finished a bite of pomegranate. "After all, he is a child still. Even though we know he is destined to an auspicious future, we need to give him time to experience his boyhood, too."

"I explained to him," went on my companion, "that Passover is the time when our ancestors, brave they were, had been detained in slavery for two-hundred years under the Pharaohs in Egypt. God promised he would release them from slavery, but not before he had visited ten plagues on Egypt to demonstrate his power. Our ancestors survived the first nine plagues; the slaying of firstborn was the tenth plague. If they could avoid the tenth plague, that swath of murder, then they could return to our homeland under God's sanction, to here, where we sit now.

"Understand, the plague was to kill the firstborn, Egyptian or Jew alike, with no distinction. Even the livestock were subject to the decree. I explained to him that the Passover stands for the freeing of the spirit from the control of the personality. It is a mental attitude in which we bridge from an old state of consciousness to a new one.

"*Elokeinu*, our God, is very sensible. He showed our people how to circumvent this event. Each household was to take an unblemished male lamb, look after it, and slaughter it at twilight four days later. Every responsible Jewish family brushed blood from the lamb onto the lintels.

This would be a symbol that would protect that home from the plague. Then the families were to roast the lamb and eat it with bitter herbs and unleavened bread. Every bit of the lamb had to be eaten and any remaining bones burned. They were to perform this ritual dressed for a journey.

"The Egyptians were terrified at this plague and pleaded the Pharaoh to hie the Jews from their land. God summoned Moses, a Jew, to lead his people out of Egypt."

"You explained well, Joseph. We must return to our work," I said as I stood. As we prepared to resume our work for the afternoon, Joseph was compelled to continue his explanation to me, although I needed none. He needed to release his thoughts. I faced him directly as I sat once more.

"I told Jesus that we celebrate that feat on the fifteenth day of Nissan each year. I think he knew that already. Our Torah tells us the celebration lasts seven days, with the first and last days as the most important ones. Symbolically, the feast represents the beginning of our harvest season.

"Chaim, I know that Jesus likes these celebrations because of their religious significance to our family and our people. That is good. As I have more time with Jesus, I will explain other of our feasts to him." Joseph picked up his tools. "Now we can resume our work."

I was impressed with Joseph and his handling of the boy.

Jesus Prays

Jesus had a singular habit that concerned me. I had observed this with my own eyes. The way Jesus prayed was a bit disconcerting. Jesus talked to God in heaven much the same way he talked to his earthly father Joseph. Can you imagine?—a boy of seven talking to God above, aloud, as if God were sitting on the chair next to him? When I told Joseph of this observation, he told me that Jesus can discourse with God for hours about every manner of subject. Why should I be surprised?

For example, I remember one morning Jesus sat quietly on a large stone in the old olive grove as I happen to walk through on my way to my day's work. I could not help but overhear him praying alone.

"Infinite Creator, for your love and your grace, for your divine perfect order, I am obliged. For your blessings and abundance, for which there is and can be no end, glory be unto you. Even as I breathe and live daily and have my being here each day below, I look my eyes unto you, Most Creative Parent, for the shower of love you bestow on me. For the birds, the fishes, the animals all, I give glory unto you, Holy Principle. Infinite and unnumbered are the stars in the sky. Without bound are the grasses and the depths of the sea. There is no end to the gift you give to me. Make me like yourself in eternal glory and receive me into your endless service on high."

He paused to meditate. Then, quietly, "Universal Spirit in heaven, give me the courage to do what is to be my task. Give me the wisdom to be strong and straight, in every place and time. Give me the patience to learn and to teach, to be, just be, and to be understood. Let me be truly helpful to mankind, all. Let me represent you, Father, in a holy manner, knowing that you sent me to this time and place. Give me the direction I need to say and to do, as you wish upon me. Let me be content to be wherever you wish me to be, because I know you go there with me. Forgiveness is your name, and mine. I am healed in every way, every day, because you allow me to be healed. I am your servant, humble and faithful. I am yours forever."

Lifting his eyes to heaven, he moved his lips wordlessly, silently in private prayer. Sweat beaded on his brow. Then, aloud quietly, "For the privilege of being a Jew, in this village, thank you. For the principle of living here, now, in this place and time, thanks be unto God the Good. Yesterday is no more and tomorrow has yet to show itself to me, and for this moment, this time of quietude, *rav todot*, thank you." He was passive for a long time before he arose to remember where he was.

To my mind, I was amazed with his maturity. How powerful he was! How astute was his understanding of his mission of this lifetime! I could only stand there, refreshing his words in my mind and thinking to myself of the flower that was blooming before my own eyes.

Reading the Scriptures

Age seven is the beginning of the Jewish formal education for boys. At his age, the boys were ripe to absorb new concepts. I knew Jesus. He was smart, and only wanted to get smarter. He already spoke and wrote and read three languages. He wanted to learn even more intricacies of the language spoken inside the Temple.

Hebrew is that language. It is an old language. The old Scriptures are written in Hebrew. Our Torah is written in Hebrew. We speak Hebrew in ceremony; it will never go away.

I cannot judge how the time passed. Before I was aware, Jesus had become a true master in the language of Hebrew. He now read aloud portions of the Scriptures. For example, yestereve at the well, people gathered around him while he read passages from the scroll of Genesis, one of the accounts of the Torah, to the populace. How entranced the people were by his reading skills! Not only did he read to them the words, but he discoursed with them by asking questions of them and answering their questions. Anyone who could read aloud did that on the Sabbath because people enjoyed sharing their insights of the Scriptures with others. It was a major activity to pass the Sabbath.

People of all ages and character demanded Jesus to read the Scriptures to them because they could not read for themselves. Some of them were illiterate—but certainly not ignorant. Jesus behaved as if he were a rabbi, teaching and explaining to them the fine points of his readings. The synagogues of the larger communities did not lack readers; folks here in Nazareth felt privileged that they had Jesus to read to them.

I could attribute his wisdom to the teaching techniques of the rabbis and chazzans. The chazzan, an officer of the synagogue, read the words aloud, and then the boys of the class repeated them in unison. Repeating is how the students learned, too, the Psalms and the Prophets.

I recall one evening after the Sabbath had ended. Jesus had finished reading part of the Scriptures to the crowd gathered and had gone to his home, for it was gathering darkness. I believe he was reading from Numbers. Joseph was present with me. "Chaim, what do you think of Jesus reading to this crowd every Sabbath? I mean, he is so conversant with every topic he touches, and he is still a child. And see how he answers every question in great detail? I was not the one to give him this knowledge."

"Joseph, friend, you and I both know the source of his understanding. Of course it is of God."

"But, the questions—"

"Yes, yes the questions. Even though some of these humble people cannot read for themselves does not mean they are spiritually empty. See how they inquire of Jesus' knowledge? See how they hunger for learning?

Do not you see how they thirst for the Truth? They turn to your son for answers. Is not that wonderful?"

"Of course it is." Joseph considered his next words. "You sit in the main courtyard in the village on *Yom HaShabbat*, the Sabbath. You hear the men discussing all of the intricacies of those oral laws and admonitions offered to Moses—those canons that are yet to be recorded. You know how much the men argue and disagree with each other on every point. Every Sabbath, it is the same. Every Sabbath, they go through the same arguments, over and over again. Every Sabbath, each man comes away knowing from his heart that he has not convinced the others that his viewpoint is the correct interpretation of the law."

"It is the nature of a Jew to be obstinate when it comes to our laws and our heritage. It is our nature to question every point, every detail. It is who we are. You know that."

"It is who we are," confirmed Joseph.

"Let me leave you with this thought, friend. On the times we gather, every Jew is a scholar. Every Jew is a philosopher. Every Jew is right in his own mind until a rabbi can interpret the laws according to the rabbi's understanding. Go. Sleep. *Ad machar*, I will greet you on the morrow."

Questioning the Laws

I was walking home from my interchange with Joseph and I felt compelled to expand on our conversation. The sun was low.

We Jews recognize the Talmud as that set of unwritten laws that Moses received on the Sinai Mountain. It is a record of Jewish law, ethics, and customs. We pass many hours and days under debate of those decrees. Many an argument is quarreled endlessly and vigorously, without reaching any conclusion except to meet the next day and do it all over again. It is one way of growing and learning with one another; I have spent many an afternoon in those debates. None of it is written on parchment or papyrus and that is why my acquaintances and I debate it so vigorously.

Even as I have been a devout Jew my entire life, I still find those laws, in all of their thousands of minute details, exceedingly difficult to comprehend in their entirety. They define in great detail every aspect of how a Jew should live his life. If I do not follow every instruction according to the written Torah or the oral Talmud, then I feel a burden of guilt hanging on my shoulder. There is an unconscious persuasion to my mind that I am required to obey every trivia.

Take for example the dietary restrictions. Ach! One of our favorite arguments concerns the consumption of sheep and goats for food. There is one Talmudic passage that is the source of many arguments within my group of friends, and it is this, as defined in the Scripture of Leviticus: "Any animal that is cloven-footed and chews the cud, such you may eat."

In my mind, I wonder how it is that certain animals can be more special than other animals. After all, are they not all of and from God? How can some animals be more chosen than others simply because they happen to possess a "more perfect" skin and fur and hooves than others? In God's eyes, all creatures are perfect. In man's eyes, some creatures are more perfect than others.

I am not one to dispute the olden regulations; I accept all that is given to us without hesitation. But even I, Chaim of Nazareth, am overwhelmed with the segregation of what we may eat from that which we may not eat. Sometimes I am confused; it is that confusion that fuels the daily arguments with my colleagues. It is all part of being a proud Jew.

If there is one thing I can understand from all of the many scrolls, it is this. Goodness and morality are the foundations of the Jewish faith. All good works and all good thoughts spring from this underpinning that is interwoven throughout the writings. Do good deeds and be righteous; those are the laws. Forgive and you are forgiven; that is the truth. It is universal law.

CHAPTER 20

1 CE

∿∪ʌ

Jesus' Dream

As I was walking one morning near the olive grove, Jesus ben Joseph ran up to me wearing an enigmatic expression. He has known me his entire life and felt he could trust me with any circumstance. I was honored that he trusted me to hold his confidence.

"Chaim, my friend, may we talk? I need an adult's advice." A youthful question showed in his face.

"Of course, anytime."

"Chaim, I had a dream last night, a disturbing one. It concerns me deeply."

"Go on." I detected that this was going to be a delicate subject.

"I dreamed that I was a grownup man. I was standing in a field of sheep, as a shepherd. The bleating of their sweet voices enchanted me, as if they were true harps in concert. In my arms I was holding a baby lamb, peaceful it was. On the ground at my feet were a dozen sheep looking up at me and the baby lamb with a questioning look, as if they knew something that I did not know and was about to learn. They must have thought that I was an ordinary Jew, about to pay my shekels to the animal sellers near the Temple to buy a lamb for the sacrifice at the altar."

"That does not sound so much out of the ordinary," I replied.

"But it was not about what I was doing; it was about what I was thinking," he said. "I was thinking that one day I will be required to do exactly that. It is written in the law. I and others will buy sacrificial lambs and give the lambs to the priests who will then kill the innocent beings for no justifiable reason other than man's ruling written on a piece of parchment. Do you not think, Chiam, that these little babies at our feet deserve to live out their lives as God intended them to do without the threat of a knife at their throats?"

"Jesus ben Joseph, it is written as law, and you know it," I tried to explain. "Let me say it another way. Sacrifice is a refining process that is constantly going on in consciousness. Every thought and act of man sets free an energy directed to God. God recognizes these thoughts and actions and that recognition relates you to God in a personal way. It is a way of purifying our body here on earth; those who do not purify themselves only delay their ultimate progress. The law dictates we do it."

"But whose law is it? Whose law? Who makes the law? Man makes law and writes it with ink, not God. God does not write. Man breaks law, not God. God's laws are immutable, absolute, and perfect in every way. There is no higher authority. But what we have, for example at a Passover feast, is a travesty to God's truth, and that truth is honoring and sanctifying life, all life, at any cost. All life is precious to God. All love is immeasurable and unlimited. These sheep are perfect expressions of that love. They have done no harm, no hurt to any man. They know only how to live as best they can, to be perfect icons of God and of love."

I sat there stupefied. His logic was perfect in every way but one. I attributed his confusion to his tender age. I had to say something. "Listen to me. Let me try to explain something to you. We have two sets of laws. We have God's laws and we have man's laws. Each set of laws has its own purpose and its own time. It is important to distinguish them apart from one another.

"God's laws are those laws given to Moses for us Jews to obey. Part of those laws describes the sacrifice the animals make on our behalf. We sacrifice the animals at the altar, or more accurately, the animals sacrifice their lives for the purpose of satisfying our laws. It is a sacrificial system. You know that. The system allows us to atone for our sins we have created against others and against ourselves. It is true that those laws require the drawing of blood and pain from animals. I suppose you could say that sacrifice is one purpose of the animals. They suffer pain to benefit us. Without the sacrifice, according to the laws, we cannot atone for the errors we create in our daily lives."

I searched for new words as I rummaged my fingers through my beard. "Scriptures teach that all people live in original sin. The way to atone the original sin is to sacrifice animals. It makes people feel good about themselves because of their imagined superiority over animals. The odor, indeed stench, of burning flesh is pleasing to God.

"As you know, your mother and your father offered two turtle doves to the priest in the Temple in Jerusalem on your fortieth day on this earth. That was the law then. It is the law now. I was there to witness that as it happened.

"'The other set of laws are those laws that man, our fellow man, wrote. Those laws describe the way we must behave when living in our society, and the penalties we must pay for disobeying those laws. Jesus ben Joseph, it is important for you to learn when to apply each set of laws.

"I have said unto you what I know. I leave you to understand what I say as best you may. Your mind is sharp as a barber's blade and you must satisfy yourself with what I tell you as being true. I cannot say it any other way."

"I will think about what you are saying."

His silence lasted not long. "Chaim, let me say it another way. The reason man sacrifices the animals is to please God according to the laws he himself wrote. It is ego that kills these angels on earth in an attempt to feel superior. Ego reigns on earth; it is responsible for famine and war and inequities of every measure. Man's laws established the tradition of the knife at the throat long ago, and it is because of that practice that the killing has become justified as necessary. It is ego that fuels war. It is ego that fuels hate. Love and murder balance on the same scale.

"Why does a man kill a living being so that he may release his transgressions? The animal knows not its purpose other than to live its simple life. Cannot man take responsibility for his own life and atone himself to God directly without having an animal as an intermediary? Why kill an animal for the mere satisfaction of contenting one's ego? Why edge God out of our lives by destroying another life? There can come no satisfaction from killing for the sake of killing.

"In our local synagogue, right here in Nazareth, I can smell the animals. I hear their bleating and bawling. I see the caged birds fluttering their wings in vain, with no place to fly. I know that they are perfect beings in God's eyes and have no need to perish before their time. All life is sacred and precious, even the fishes in the rivers and the worms in the earth. Each life has its appointed journey to complete. Each life has its mission to accomplish, mistakes to make, and results to sustain. Who are we, as mere humans, to interrupt their progress on their appointed sojourn? I do not understand."

"But Jesus ben Joseph, are you saying that we as humans do not have the power to do God's work? What can we do? How are we to carry out our long-standing traditions of sacrifice at the altar?" I wanted to know.

"Chaim, I know that I am still young and learning, but this I know. Love is all there is. Forgiveness is all there is. Service to others is all there is. They are all the same. Give peace and you receive peace. Love begets love. Do you understand? If you know God—and God is everywhere—then you cannot know fear, for love is the opposite of fear. There is no other way. Every animal and every person has a divine purpose, and God gives us the meaning of that purpose every day. Killing innocent animals serves only to placate man's pride. If man could but empty his ego of all vainness and instead fill it with God's love, then we would have no need for laws. I say pray rather than kill.

"And what I say is not only for the animals. My message applies to all of my fellow mankind. How can one man feel the need to kill another? How can one government feel the need to exert its authority over another, as the Romans are now repressing us Jews? When does the coercion stop? When does the killing stop?"

"Jesus ben Joseph, dear child," I responded. "I have explained your dream as best I can. Now go, be with your playmates. Be a child of the earth while you are able to do so."

But he could not just go away. His dream and his conversation with me gave the boy more ideas to consider. He came to me later.

"Chaim, suppose, just suppose for a moment, how it would feel if we did not eat any flesh."

"You mean do not eat any meat?" I questioned in astonishment. "*Ani loh mevin*, I do not understand what you say."

"No meat, no fish, no animal at all. Do you think that I could follow such a diet if I wanted?"

"Of course that would be impossible!" I retorted. "*Lo yitachen*, it is not possible. No Jew has ever done so!"

"Why could I not follow such a plan? What would make such a habit so terrible in God's eyes? I think that God would smile favorably on me if I avoided the scorching of flesh in order to preserve an animal's life. As we discussed, every animal is precious, every animal is a glorious design to God, and who are we to destroy it? I ask you, who are we to destroy God's creation?"

"But Jesus ben Joseph, you know we are required to sacrifice animals for our feasts; it is written in the law."

"Again I say, laws are written by man. God alone creates life and only God can take life. God's creation has no beginning and no end. God overflows with love and the love is the creation we enjoy. Do we dare pretend we are larger than God by presuming that just because we wrote it onto parchment or papyrus, that it is law?"

Jesus wrinkled his forehead and turned away from my gaze. Our dialogue was over for the day. He struggled, I could tell, with what he had thought and what he had said aloud. The boy is strong in spirit and I know he will do what is right. All I could do was to agree with the boy. His wisdom surpasses mine. I distinguish that he is a brave soul, alone and above the thought of the Torah and all of its tiny details. His thinking goes beyond that of his peers; his thoughts are above those of many of his wise elders.

Even as our conversation finished, I had many thoughts swirling through my thick head.

What was Jesus ben Joseph thinking when he brought up such a subject?
How could he even consider severing the law as it is so dictated?
What would the Temple priests think of such an absurd proposal?
Would my friends—my Jewish friends—think of following Jesus' plan?
If they did, how long would they chase such a strange scheme?
Ach! Some days I cannot follow that boy's swirling mind.

The Butchers

Our history is rich with tradition and, may I say, superstition? The precious scrolls give proof to that.

The priests in our Temple in Jerusalem, and indeed any temple, were crude butchers. They took ten percent of any sacrifice for themselves and gave the rest back to the people, as if they could extract their tithe from anyone who brought a sacrifice to them. They did not hunger.

Priests used platters of silver to collect the blood and then sold it to the nearby farmers to use as fertilizer. If people did not live close to the Temple, they used a local temple or place nearby that the priest designated as a sacred place for their ceremony. The belief was that God was always angry, and the people had to appease God constantly.

Worshipers bought their sacrifice at the gates of the Temple from sacrifice sellers. The sacrifice sellers accepted only shekels for payment. If a worshiper had only a denarius, the Roman coin equal to one day's wages, he had to exchange it for Hebrew shekel. Much commerce happened before worship began; money changers and priest-butchers prospered.

CHAPTER 21

2 CE

〜〜〜

Living in Nazareth

At age eight, Jesus began to take on physical traits that would carry him into adulthood. He looked like his mother, but his face lacked the smoothness of her face. His hair was the color of carob beans, more brown than hers. He was tall for his age. His countenance was swarthy; his build was slender. His eyes were a soft brown and his lashes were long. His nose was strong.

School in Nazareth was a serious matter for all boys. After mastering Deuteronomy, the boys went on to master the other books of the law, including the Scriptures of the Prophets and the Psalms. It was normal that the schoolroom had no scrolls. Reading scraps of Scriptures and parts of parchments, whatever was available to them, was the accepted method of learning. The boys repeated aloud what the chazzan dictated.

During the summer months of Tammuz, Av, and Elul, the hours spent in school were reduced so that the boys could devote more of their time to prepare for the upcoming harvests. Work was never complete in the house or in the fields. Men and women worked together from dawn to dusk to do all that needed to be done.

Living in Nazareth was a blessing for the boy. Nazareth, located not far from roads carrying travelers and caravans to every destination, is situation in just the right locale between the hills on east and west and the arid lands to the north and south. Jesus had no inhibitions that deterred him from meeting and speaking with strangers; daily he met and exchanged ideas with travelers on the roads. He especially yearned to talk to anyone traveling to or from Jerusalem. Starting a conversation with anyone was for Jesus an opportunity to expand his sense of social understanding. His fluency in languages gave him little hindrance to learning the ways of the foreigners.

He spent time working in his father's shop where tradesmen and patrons conducted business.

One day as Joseph and Jesus worked together in Joseph's shop crafting a table for a neighbor, Jesus said to his father, "Even though I have only eight years, I feel rich to know so many kinds of people. I mingle with Jews and Gentiles. I converse with old men and young children. I see men who are rich and those who are not rich, even destitute. Lame, sick, blind—all of them I love and accept. All are perfect in God's mind. All are flawless. When I begin my life's work, I will be equipped to teach as my Father in heaven allows me to do. I appreciate all that you and mother have exposed to me."

Jesus studied the blossoming of the sunset. "Each man glows in the light of the Father. Each man is a spark of the great divinity of God's image. Each man I love."

Jesus learned to love nature as a boy. Joseph took his family on Sabbath afternoons to the surrounding countryside and to the summits of the nearby hills. To the far north towered Mount Hermon and its perpetual snowcap. To the east receded the Jordan Valley, and beyond that, Mountains of Moab. Of course, to the west sprawled the mighty Mediterranean Sea. From atop the summits, too, they all studied the wending lengths of caravan trains as they found their way around Nazareth. Jerusalem, they knew, was south.

These outings with his father intrigued Jesus and his siblings, for it was then that they together were able to observe the animals and flowers in their full beauty. Some of Jesus' fondest early memories—for we discussed this very subject many times—were of the vastness and complexity of the natural world around him. Hearing him talk now, in the symbolized way he does, surely was a result of those times. It was as if using straightforward words was simply too elemental for Jesus' complex mind. Using metaphors evolved as that way of releasing his multifaceted intellect. The metaphors he expressed allowed his listeners to see in their minds' eyes a more vivid account of the anecdote he was relating. Those who wanted to learn would understand his words and those who did not want to learn would not understand. He answered a question by asking a question.

Ach! Why does that child Jesus speak so, as he does? When his words come clearly, they are blessings to my ears. But then there are times that his use of metaphors makes understanding more difficult to my mind.

Jesus Teaches

It was two days ago, in the lane behind Joseph's house, that I overheard Jesus speaking with a beggar beseeching alms.

"Child, have mercy on me," cried the disheveled-looking man. "Look at me—I have no food to eat. I wear rags upon my back. And I have no pallet to rest my head at night. It is this day I ask you for a shekel."

"I will bring you bread and some bits of fish from my family's table. Know, man of love, that you have all your needs met this day and all days. Do you not know that the Father holds us in the palm of his hand, knowing each need we require? Do you not know how each fish in the sea knows how to swim and breathe the water? Each bird in the sky grows his feathers faithfully perfect. And you too, star of God's love, have all you need. Look within, at your heart, to find the stillness that will feed your soul and bring you the joy that you are. It is there; look, seek, and find."

"But, still, I hunger."

"The light within you will slake the hunger that is only of the earth. The light will show you the way to the Light of eternal Truth. You are fulfilled, friend. You are peace at hand."

"I will consider your words."

"Shalom unto you."

Ilan's Dream

Jesus, I call to you. Do you hear me? I am here, in my stall behind the house.

Jesus: I do. Is it you, Ilan, who calls unto me? Speak so that I may hear your words in my head. Speak so that I may understand what it is that you say unto me. I hear the anguish in your voice.

I am Ilan. You know I am to be with you into your man's years. I am to give you service, as my gift to you. It is my duty to await you until you finish your learning and your travels, and return to Nazareth as a teacher of men. I will serve Mary and Joseph humbly until your return.

Jesus: You are to be blessed, my friend. You are loyal to me and I am grateful for your words. Now, speak.

Principal of All Humanity, here is my message. I had a dream yestereve. I dreamed that you and I were in a plaza with frenzied people all around. I was carrying you on my back, yet I felt not your weight, as you were floating above me, with me. People were throwing their garments onto the road as we approached them, as if I were not to touch the cobbles. They strew petals of every kind of blossom. They sprinkled the lanes before us with fragrances and flowers. They waved fronds of palm trees. They prayed and they wept. And they sang halleluiahs to your name.

Jesus: I visualize your dream, loved one. I am there with you, seeing the cross on your back, scratching your ears as you like me to do. I know the meaning of that illusion and I accept what I see. You, my friend, will understand its meaning when that blessed event comes to pass. I cannot change its meaning; I cannot stop it from happening. Riding on your back will fulfill the prophecy written in our Scriptures.

You are not to stop it from happening; you are to be one and the same with it. You are to allow the God of Life to flow through you, then as now, and to be one with the Spirit. It is so, and so we let it be.

Jesus: Benedictions to you, dear Ilan, for your wise words. We journey together.

CHAPTER 22

3 CE

∿〜〜∿

Learning about Life

School for the nine-year-old Jesus was more than sitting on a bench listening to the chazzan recite Scriptures. The chazzan gave him a broad theological and intellectual basis. Because some concepts were beyond the chazzan, he studied on his own initiative. He explored the world of mathematics. He marveled at the precise relationships between numbers, speeds, distances, proportions, angles and lines, and all things arithmetical.

He did not stop with numbers. He probed the minds of his teachers, fellow students, neighbors, and parents with questions of geography, science, astronomy, weather, animal husbandry, philosophy, commerce and trade, fishing, biology, religion, and history. His mind was as a sponge, waiting to be filled. He probed others for ideas on many subjects. He studied the skies and the weather, he learned Hebrew and Greek history, he learned to fish and hunt with all of his mind and heart. He learned that fish represent living ideas—ideas in which there are great possibilities of increase. Fish characterize the inexhaustible, everywhere present abundance. After all, he was to be a fisher of men.

He was fascinated by the vast numbers of luminaries in the night sky and by the transition of the moon and the sun across the horizon. He never did tire of learning about the constellations and the myths and stories associated with each one. I remember how many times he supplicated of passing strangers to tell him of what they remembered of the triple conjunction of Jupiter-Saturn in that very year he was born; his questions were many.

It was Jesus who formed a boys' chorus in his part of the village. I remember how melodic his voice was; it was as an angel's. The local boys had no choice but to follow Jesus, as he was so enthralling and mesmerizing when he sang and he could only but encourage them to follow him. They dared not perform on the Sabbath, but on other evenings of the week, after their chores were completed, they serenaded citizens near the well and in the inn.

This is the time that the chazzan implemented the assignment to each boy in which he was to select a special text from the Scriptures. This text was to be as a beacon of light to help guide the boy as he proceeded with his studies, and to act as a rule to follow that would formulate the thinking of his later life. Jesus chose text from one of his favorite prophets, Isaiah. "The spirit of the Lord is upon me, for the Lord has anointed me; he has sent me to bring good news to the meek, to bind up the brokenhearted, to proclaim liberty to the captives, and to release the prisoners."

A nearby neighbor—her name was Sarah, meaning, "Lady" or "Princess"—held possession of a fine harp in her home. A beautiful instrument it was. I need not say that Jesus was attracted to it. Sarah could not help but offer lessons on playing it to the boy. As with everything else that caught his attention, the harp, too, was a lure. With only a few lessons, he had become skilled and could improvise to the point of attracting the neighbors to the door to listen and wonder at how the boy could play such beautiful harmonies.

My dear friend Joseph and his wife were the greatest teachers for Jesus. Besides learning to milk the goat and make cheese, gather eggs, and bake bread, he learned to weave on Mary's loom. He was as talented at weaving as was Mary.

However, it was in his home that he learned the greatest lessons in morality and spirituality. He was able to synthesize the philosophies of the Jews, the Gentiles, the Babylonians, and the Greeks into one coherent, all-encompassing view of humanity.

Frustration

It was during his formative years that often Jesus became bored with his chazzan. Watching him, I could tell that this was happening. Many times, I would see him wander away from the classrooms and his playmates to seclude himself in neighboring fields and groves for the purpose of praying and meditating. How could he not do so? He was so closely bound to the Heavenly Father that it was only natural that he desire to commune with the Absolute Good as deeply and as often as he could. I knew this because, to end my curiosity about what he did on those frustrating moments when he made himself withdraw from his friends, I oft followed him secretly. One day, he wandered down the wadi to the drying streambed and sat on a large boulder.

He thought he was alone. "Yeshi," he spoke aloud to the trees, "when will you learn that the chazzan is a simple man? He can teach me only what he knows. I need to learn more than what he knows, indeed, more than what any man can teach me. I need the wisdom of the Most High to come to me."

He stood and kicked the rock at his feet. "More than that, I need to bring into my being all of those teachings and have them at my tongue-tip, so that I can apply them to the crowds of people who seem to assemble to me. I need to know what to say, how to say it, when to say it. I need experience. I crave experience, but do not have it today. I am impatient with myself."

He picked up a flat stone and flung it hard against the trunk of a cypress. Sitting down, he resumed. "The chazzan is doing only what he can do. He is a good teacher to me. He knows only so much in his limited world of materialism. I crave the knowledge of all the Scriptures. I crave what they cannot provide to me. I crave, I crave. I am dissatisfied at my pace of learning.

"Yeshi, be patient with yourself, for you are only a young boy, younger than a blooming flower in Nissan. Give yourself time to grow, to play, to make mistakes. Give yourself the time you need to become the Messiah that you are. All will happen when it is the right time."

He stood and kicked a stone into the muddy water, then picked up another and threw it after the first. "I feel discouraged that I cannot learn faster. I want to attain all the wisdom there is to know from my teachers. I want to learn how to speak in parables and to use symbolism fruitfully.

I want to be a healer now—today. All I can do is play at my work, and that does not satisfy me. If I am to be the Prince of Peace in the world, I want to know all there is to know." Another stone. "I want to know, now."

I watched him walk slowly up the hill with his head bowed, as if in prayer.

From my distant vantage point, I watched as he turned around and threw yet another stone into the water. This time it was with great effort, as if he were expelling all the confined anger inside of him. He needed to drive the frustration out of his mind and his body. I was happy for him.

Watching Jesus throw the rocks into the water reminded me that, because God made every tree, animal, rock, and living being in nature, why should not God be everywhere? Why should not God be inside every part of everything, even the living and the non-living? How can anything exist apart from God?

Because the presence of God is everywhere, just like the invisible air I breathe, I know that all things are infused with his spirit. How can they not be? Ach! I must know that I, a man, am smarter than a donkey. And I know that a donkey is smarter than an olive tree. But each creation of God has intelligence in its own way, in its own time, all of the time. The animals sacrifice themselves as food and for the service they give to my brethren and me. The trees are beautiful because of the shade they afford and of the fruit they yield. Joseph would remind me that the trees contribute lumber so that he may provide for his family. Rocks are beautiful in their own way and have a place to serve the people and the animals, as roads and as jewelry and as tools—and as simple forms of beauty.

4 CE

A Lesson in Patience

Jesus reveled in modeling in clay. He modeled anything that could be modeled. Especially favorite to Jesus were the animals. His likeness of fishes, goats, donkeys, and other animals were particularly striking to the real thing. He loved to get his hands dirty and busy with the forming of faces and facial expressions of the animals. He seemed to know what the animals felt and he transferred those feelings to his models. On other days, he would pace to the edge of town to mold a copy of the distant landscape, capturing the hilltops and trees. How he did what he did with his fingers, I do not know.

One day the ten-year-old confided in me about one of his classmates. "Chaim, a boy in my class—his name is Yaniv, meaning, "He Will Prosper"—seems not to know what to do with the modeling clay. He seems to struggle when he uses it."

"Give me an example, Jesus ben Joseph," I prompted.

"The first time he tried to sculpt a goat like mine, he made it too moist and the clay melted into a puddle on the table where we sat.

"The second time he tried to sculpt a fish like mine, he added not enough water and it dried and fractured into many pieces.

"The third piece he tried to copy from mine was a small hare. It appeared to be perfect in every way, but he accidentally knocked it onto the floor where it broke. He nearly came to tears."

"What an interesting story, Jesus ben Joseph. Is there more?" I asked.

"Yes, this is where it gets intriguing. After I comforted him for his misfortunes, he went on to sculpt a donkey. It was perfect. It was perfect. He finally learned to add the right amount of water to the clay—not too much and not too little. He learned how to let it dry properly. He learned to be careful with his hands so as not to bump his art onto the floor. He learned to be patient with his work. He learned the value of persistence. I think he learned how to sow beautiful thoughts into his artwork and to be fruitful, as he went on to create many more sculptures. I think he will go on to become a skillful craftsman."

"That is a good story, Jesus ben Joseph. I think the lesson we learned from it is that everything we do in life has a lesson to learn, and every lesson is valuable. There is always more to learn," I concluded.

He smiled at me. "Yes, Chaim, there are so many lessons to learn. Yaniv learned his."

I thought we were finished with our conversation.

"There is more to this story." Jesus ben Joseph had something further to say. "After my friend Yaniv took his clay pieces to his home, I returned to the art room at the school and picked up the figurines I molded and broke them into many pieces. As you know, Chaim, I do not want to ever leave any trace of my existence on this earth. I do not want to leave any form of writing, even in the sands. I do not want to leave any trace of my earthly sojourn. If for some reason out of my realm something remains, for example the furniture I helped to build in my father's workshop, I know that it will crumble with time into dust. I am to be here only temporarily in this physical form. I do not want people to make graven images of anything I may have touched. I am to leave nothing behind other than lessons for humanity. Do you know that? Do you understand that? Forgiveness and love are my lessons."

Once again I had nothing to say.

His artistic abilities as a child did not end with molding clay. He sensed a real connection to the earth, as he would draw depictions on any rock wall or flat surface with charcoal. Earth and charcoal are natural compliments to each other. Charcoal was easy enough to find; any partially burned stick in a fire served as a drawing stick. His likenesses of faces, animals, or the landscapes were uncannily close to the real thing, especially considering that charcoal is not easy to work. Nevertheless, Jesus made it work to his advantage. He had an unexplainable talent in creating realistic artwork. Even so and without regret, he would allow his friends to admire his work, and then smudge the artworks until they were unrecognizable.

Jesus' education was not limited to academic subjects. On nearby farms, with his father's permission, he helped to drive the oxen when furrowing the land in the spring. In helping to plant the seeds, Jesus learned that the seeds, when planted into the land, represented the blossoming of concepts and ideas. It is only when thoughts blossom affirmatively that humankind will thrive and prosper. In the autumn, he helped the men to harvest the grains into the storehouses. He felt the need to learn something about every trade and occupation.

I remember one month in the summertime, when the farming jobs were slow, he apprenticed himself in a silversmith's shop. He helped to smith the ore into rings and bracelets. Is his talent without end? True to his form, after he had finished forming the jewelry, he melted the pieces he had crafted into a small mound of silver so that the silversmith could use the metal again.

Sepphoris

North and west of Nazareth three miles was a small city named Sepphoris. It was built on top of a hill and it was one of many outposts of the Roman government. Although it was a Roman city in its core, the Greek culture influenced its architecture and daily activities. Sepphoris was one city within a network of ten Roman cities called the Decapolis. Decapolis is a Greek word that means, "Ten Cities." The Roman leaders residing in Sepphoris kept in constant contact with the leaders of other Roman cities in and around Galilee.

Joseph and Mary did not go there together, although Joseph and Jesus did walk there on occasion.

The city was most clean and orderly. The cardo, with its shops, vendors, and merchants, saw to that. Hawkers in the market sold vegetables, jewelry, fabrics, dried yarns, trinkets, scarves, sandals, and any number of other accessories. Booksellers sold bound books and loose-bound scrolls. The cardo hosted a large open-aired amphitheater that invited spectator sports, games, and displays. It had baths, theaters, gymnasiums, schools, libraries, and marketplaces. Oddly, the cardo stretched itself in a north-south direction. It was in the amphitheater that the Gentiles worshiped as they pleased. An impressive marble temple was dedicated to the Greek mythological gods.

Sepphoris consumed assorted resources. Produce and every kind of food and wine found their way to the city. Stone, water, and wood too, served their purposes with abandon there. As in any community, local politicians spread their power, influence, and wealth into every corner of the city like water filling an empty cistern. The other end of the social scale promoted the beggars, bandits, and insurgents. The poorest sold themselves into slavery for the sake of eschewing constant hunger. Their labor allowed the rich to become even richer.

The hippodrome within the city allowed the populace to watch the horse races. The hippodrome was set out on the slope of a hill, and the ground taken from one side served to form the embankment on the other side where the spectators sat. One end of the hippodrome was semicircular, and the other end was square. Below the square end was the portico and below that on a lower level was where the horses and chariots were kept.

Jesus, I observed when I walked there with him and his father, was tolerant of the activities in Sepphoris. Judaism, after all, was the primary religion in our land, not Hellenism. Overall, the Jewish populations despised the Greek amphitheater because the crude games and gross competitions of strength held there were against all of the

Jewish religious and ethical standards. The Greeks, he knew, loved to adorn their cities with statues and busts of their leaders. The Greeks, too, placed high emphasis on athletic competition and superiority. As a contrast, Jesus knew that the Jews preferred plain facades on the outside of their structures while consigning their architectural talents to the insides, much as people are plain looking on the outside while developing and exhibiting intricate feelings and emotions on the inside. He understood this dichotomy between Jew and Gentile and all of the related complexities that resulted from that relationship. He knew intuitively that his future mission would not be limited to the Jewish world, but would encompass all of humanity.

Nevertheless, Jesus was impressed with the athletics conducted there. In any athletic occasion, Jesus participated enthusiastically and with all of his efforts. He was a strong young man. His muscles were powerful and sinewy for his age, and his mind was one to meet any competition directly. He always promoted, in his own way, athletics, games, and swimming as a means of developing strong character in men.

Jesus was especially strong in playing a kicking game. The boys stuffed a scrap of leather with goat hair and sewed the seams. The object of the game was to see who could kick the makeshift ball the most times between two rocks. Sometimes the boys chose partners and played as a team against another team. Another activity that kept the boys occupied was swimming in the small lakes nearby. Every one of his friends could swim well enough to be at ease in the water. Like playing with the ball, swimming gave competition to the boys in the form of finding who could swim the fastest and who could hold his breath the longest. A real trick was to catch a fish only by using their bare hands.

Still, he could not release from his mind thoughts of the momentous work that lie ahead of him. Far-reaching plans and a sense of enlightenment paraded continuously through his heart and mind. Even Joseph and Mary did not know of the near-turmoil swirling in his head; on the outside, he looked like a normal pre-adolescent Nazarene boy.

CHAPTER 23

5 CE

Nearly a Man

Joseph's workshop was a model for other craftsmen in Nazareth. Hanging neatly over the workbench were his augers, saws, awls, and hammers. Unused lumbers and fresh logs stood in the corner. The room smelled clean from the wood shavings on the floor. One of Joseph's favorite woods was cypress, a common tree around here. Cypress is strong and grows tall, having roots that sink deep into the earth. Joseph used that wood when he wanted to create a quality piece of furniture.

I saw a parallel between Joseph's workshop and Jesus' personality. Both were filled with many tools, each to be used in its proper time and place, and with the right amount of wisdom.

As age eleven, Jesus became more and more aware of the unusual nature and character of his life's mission. Long ago he had dismissed any concept of becoming a fisherman or a blacksmith or a stonecutter or a shop merchant. If he had to choose a career to become a productive citizen or to provide an income for his family, it would have been carpentry like his father. He knew that making a vocation for himself was only to be secondary to his primary mission of Savior and Master Teacher. He was becoming conscious to his feelings and emotions that expressed themselves in his dealings with his family and others around him. I remember several conversations with my companion Joseph in which he described Jesus' erupting feelings.

129

"Chaim, my friend, Jesus is no longer my son as I know him. He has matured to a level beyond me. He is a man in many ways," proffered Joseph. "Remember, he will be eligible to become a citizen of Israel next year."

"I know that," I replied. "I have watched him grow up, remember? I feel that he is as much my son as he is yours."

"I feel the same way."

"I cannot tell you how to nurture him to his adulthood," I answered. "I can only offer him *bracha*, prayer and unheard guidance, as I do every day. I pray for you and Mary, too."

"Thank you, my friend."

"Joseph," I went on, "bless the boy and allow him to grow as he is meant to grow. I know that you and Mary will give him the guidance you can; that is all you can do. The rest is up to God."

Jesus went on to show a marked preference for the companionship of his elders. He did not stop talking about religion, politics, history, and economics. His keen sense of social activism impressed his peers and elders alike. It did not matter if he were in his own home or in someone else's home, he always steered the conversation to the direction he wanted. He was a born teacher and could not help himself from functioning in that faculty.

At home Jesus found himself being more and more responsible for the daily care of his younger siblings. Joseph worked long hours in his carpenter shop; Mary appreciated every assistance Jesus gave to her in managing the household. When he was not at home, Jesus spent time at the caravan supply shop where he learned news from foreign countries.

The chazzan, seeing the serious advancement of his most promising pupil, gave one evening each week of his time in Jesus' home to help him master the intricacies of the Hebrew tongue. Jesus was determined to know all of the fine points associated with the Scriptures, even those whose meaning was hidden in intricate phrasing.

6 CE

The End of School

Jesus was now twelve years old, one year before becoming a man under Jewish tradition. Age twelve was the year he would become a citizen of Israel. His schooling continued briskly; he excelled in every subject. When not in school, he worked in his father's shop by helping with the sale of the pieces of furniture Joseph had made. I felt honored to be in a select small group of people who knew of Jesus' mission so intimately. His parents and I did our utmost to protect him from public scrutiny in every way. Even though all knew him and his reputation, we tried hard to protect him from anything that could cause him harm. His safety was our first concern. He was well-tolerant of all people, light-hearted, and full of energy.

I know that Jesus himself had a full grasp on what he was to do. He understood fully the extent of his dual nature. To occupy himself even more, he increasingly took on more responsibilities at home. His parents expected him to help with the upbringing and care of his younger brothers and sister. Jesus was especially responsible for helping with the formal studies of his younger siblings. Since Jesus was fond of music, he took extra care in teaching lute and tambourine to them.

Jesus graduated this year from his school in the synagogue, with outstanding admiration. His teachers were proud of this child of most high. They had already begun to formulate plans for his further education in the renowned Hebrew academies. Jesus had other ideas. The gentle undercurrent of rebellion within him held sway over his mind. He did not care to study more in a formal setting with elder rabbis. He wanted instead to grow and learn on his own schedule. His graduation allowed him that privilege of setting his own mind to gain knowledge in the way he felt best for his own development.

As the students and the chazzans and the proud parents congregated at the door of the school on that concluding day of Jesus' formal education, and after the felicitations had been offered by all, the chief chazzan approached Jesus. At first the chazzan hesitated in asking his question, for he knew not what nature of response Jesus would offer. Then, "Most prominent student of mine, as a final gift of your graduating class, I would be most gratified if you would offer a prayer of thanksgiving so that we might learn one more lesson of truth."

Jesus looked around the gathering and considered. "We have learned in our school that prayer is a way of departing from daily life. It is a way to approach the spiritualized individuality God gave to each of us and commune with *Av SheBaShamayim*, the Father in heaven. Prayer is the breath of the soul and teaches us to be persistent in our attempts to ascertain the Father's will."

Then he took a deep breath and closed his eyes and said with authority, "Our creative Parent, who is the center of the universe, bestow upon us, your students, your nature and give to us your character. Make us the sons of your grace and allow us to glorify your name through our eternal thoughts and deeds. Blessed are you Holy Spirit who forms the light and creates the darkness, who makes peace and creates everything; who in mercy gives light to the earth and to all those who dwell upon it and in goodness. Day by day you renew the works of your creation. You teach us the statutes of life; have mercy upon us and teach us. Enlighten our eyes in the law and cause our hearts to cleave to your commandments. Unite our hearts to love. Your name is everlasting and there is no God beside you. We are all one with the One. We all are love, embodied in flesh. We are all peace unto peace. And for the earth, let there be peace on the earth."

He could not stop without adding, "Sustain us this day in our progress along the path of truth. Deliver us from evil and sinful transgressions. Lead us step by step with your generous hand through this earthly existence. And when our end comes, receive us into your bosom with joyous and faithful charity. It is not our desires but yours that will be done."

His prayer was so simple that even I could have said it. But it was his power that gave it the energy it needed to do its work. Jesus ben Joseph showed us the way to love and live so richly.

Sojourn to Jerusalem

Having been graduated from a formal school and having reached the age of young manhood were credentials in abundance to allow him to travel to Jerusalem with his parents to celebrate the Passover. For me, the sojourn to Jerusalem was just as exciting as it was the first time I went with my own parents. The noise, the exhilaration, the confusion, the smells—all added to the importance of making the trip every year. I knew that from observing Jesus since his birth, he, too, would thrill at the experience. What would make his first trip different from the first trip of other children is the inherent knowledge and import of his looming responsibilities.

Would it not be ironic if Jesus' first journey would also be my last? Each year I found it harder to muster the energy required to go. Jewish law does not require the journey annually, but I have not missed one year in all of my six decades, save for the years before my parents took me at age twelve. I shall not miss this one. I want to relay my story as long as I can.

Mary considered the consequence of taking her other children with her on the trip. She knew how demanding the trip would be on them because of the difficulty of travel and being away from their playmates and schools. Her friend Chava, meaning, "First Woman," offered to care for the children while she and Joseph and Jesus were away. Mary cried tears of joy as Chava took charge of them at the last minute before they departed. "*Al tedag,* do not worry about your children, my friend Mary. I love them as I love my own, as you know, and I will take good care of them while you are away in Jerusalem. We will be fine; you need not worry. Be away; go with your family and enjoy the Passover feast."

The journey consumed four days. A man could walk it in three days if he had no wife to look after. On occasion, to pass the time, Joseph and Mary made conversation with the other families traveling to Jerusalem for the Passover feast. They talked about the year they trekked to Jerusalem for the first time. It was twelve years ago in Elul when Mary gave birth to Jesus.

The Tree of Life

Along the way, we kept look for a favorite grove of trees. Of course, we all knew where it stood along the side of the road. We wanted to find the grove of Jerusalem Date trees and rest in its shade. The Jerusalem Date tree is a marvelous handiwork of God's majesty. The tree is rumored, with more than enough evidence, to possess magnificent healing qualities. It is said to cure a wide range of ailments, including malaria, toothache, and those illnesses that drain away a body's bulk and strength. I remember years ago, the physician administered dried leaves of the tree to my dying wife, but to no avail.

Ancient Hebrews called the tree the "Tree of Life" because of the high nutrition found in its fruit and the shade shared by its long, leafy branches. Arabs said there were as many uses for the tree as there were days in a year. Greek architects modeled their iconic columns on the tree's tall thin trunk and its curling, bushy top. The Romans called it *Phoenix dactylifera*, meaning, "The Date-Bearing Phoenix." It appears never to die and always sustains itself in the desert when all other plant life perishes.

Remembering the Star

The month was Nissan—Passover month. We journeyed together south toward Samaria. We avoided Samaria proper, for we disliked dealing with the Samaritans because of a long and undistinguished history between Galilee and Samaria. Ach! I cannot explain fully the details because time has blurred my memory, but I do know that it centers on the separation of the northern and southern Jewish kingdoms. Our path led us around Mount Gilboa and into the Jordan Valley.

What a sight the Jordan River was! Its gleaming radiance could only make my heart dance with wonderment at its beauty. I absorbed its beauty now because I knew as it found its way through the desert, it lost its charm and it eventually dumped itself into the Salt Sea. But for now, Jesus and his friends were quick to wade into the river for brief refreshment from the mid-day heat before their parents could chide them to come again to the caravan. Blooming bluebeards, irises, tulips, Madonna lilies, narcissus, and other flowers lent fragrance to the otherwise stink of camels and donkeys bearing their humans' burdens. The flowers added a pleasant view to the eye.

God's voice speaks to me all through the day. God demonstrates beauty, love, and grace through the magnificent works all around us.

Our travels were never dull. I loved being friends with this holy family. As we sat in a breeze under a Jerusalem Date tree to refresh ourselves, Joseph began to tell a story to young Jesus. I listened intently.

"Jesus, my son, I want again to retell the account of the star that rose over the horizon when you were born. It was such a beautiful part of your birth story and your mother and I always love to recount the memory."

"Joseph, I remember that night!" Mary's eyes lit up.

"It was as if the darkness caught on fire, a wonderful fire."

"*Aba*, father, yes, please tell me again the description of lights in the sky."

"The brightness was more than bright. It was dazzling, intense, and brilliant in every sense. It seemed to shimmer, as if it were shining through the waves of heat over the sands. It could not stop its glow if it wanted to. It was pure."

"There must be more to it than that?" the boy asked.

"Oh, yes, there was. In fact, there were three such occurrences that year. Three. The histories I hear repeated in the streets say there was only one star. I know better. I know there were three."

"Joseph," Mary wanted to know, "how did the star come to rest itself over the grotto where we passed the night?"

"That is the work of God's hand. I cannot explain that with my voice. Only God can answer that question. Maybe it only appeared to rest over our grotto."

"But then, father," Jesus queried, "are you sure the star appeared because of my birth? Could it be a coincidence that my birth and the star somehow happened as a grand coincidence?"

"No. No, it was not. It was meant to be that way and all the other stars in the sky could not have stopped it from happening."

"Yeshua, my child, the star was there because it had been predicted in the Scriptures. You know that." Mary passed the water skin to Joseph's parched lips. "Everything that night was perfect, as it is now and will be forever. All is perfect and all is in perfect time. The star had to be that way."

"Should we continue?" urged the young man. "The donkey awaits."

What a privilege it is for me to serve this fine family. I serve obediently and with great honor in my humble capacity. How could I do otherwise? How could I not serve Jesus and his family with all of my heart and energy? This road is well-traveled. I am careful not to trip on a stone. I am careful not to step in a cleft in the road. I only hope that I can serve Jesus for many more years. I am content in my role.

The fourth day's travel brought the caravans to the hills overlooking the great Holy City of Jerusalem. There was one particular hill overlooking the Jordan that I love deeply. It was where I stood with my own father years before. Each time I climb its rocky path, my eyes water because of the fond memories I had of the first time I saw the city. I knew that Jesus ben Joseph, even now, was forming that very same memory in his mind. I was so happy for him, so proud to know him and his parents as my friends.

Strength. Even though the roadway along that rock-strewn hill was dusty and dry, the view afar was very different. Bathing and surrounding the crown of Jerusalem was a distant landscape of pale green. The flourishing greenery gave me the strength to be what I was about—to be free from weakness. The foliage reminded me that God is the source of all nature and the source of all that is good and right. To me, the foliage represented strength of character and power to resist temptation. And with that strength, I recognized my being was nothing more than pure inner light.

Strength is more than physical exertion, force, or pressure. Strength originates in Spirit and it is in finding stillness that anyone can find strength. Silence brings confidence, security, patience, and calmness.

Chapter 24

6 CE

The Mount of Olives

East of Jerusalem, but before Bethany, was the Mount of Olives. Halfway down the hill from the peak was a large necropolis. Joseph knew its deepest meaning. Just seeing it from a distance stirred his emotions greatly. Studying its immense layout gave cause to any man to regard his very mortality. How long could any man live in the flesh on this earth? How vulnerable were he and Mary—nay, any man—to stand the test on the road of life? Surely he did not understand all there was to understand about that vast tract of land. He would be sure to pass this understanding on to his son when the right time came. If he could make his wishes come true, he would aspire that Mary and he be interred together in and under that eminent grove of olive trees, on the side stretching up toward the summit of the hill.

Thinking back, I recall that Joseph stood in awe as he studied that sprawling olive grove for the first time. He recalled from the teachings his father gave to him that this grove of olive trees held special meaning. He remembered that the Mount of Olives connoted an exalted state of mind, a high place in consciousness. He had learned in his boyhood that the olive tree could live for many centuries, through wind and drought, and without sufficient water.

The Time is Nigh

On the night before the Passover was to begin, Jesus had a dream. He wanted to express his concern about the dream with an adult, but he knew that his parents might not understand him or his dream fully. He sought me out of the crowd, and we talked as friends.

"Chaim, friend of my father, I had a dream last night I cannot rid of my mind. I need to share it with someone," Jesus began.

"Shalom. Speak, friend," I answered.

"For months now I have been swept over by enlightened forces I do not fully understand. The flood tides of love and emotions for my fellow man do not stop engulfing me, Chaim. I feel pity for the vast unaware masses of people who are here for their cleansing. I think that is why I had my dream last night." Jesus kicked at a stone in the path. "Help me with this one, my friend."

"I will try my best, Jesus ben Joseph."

"There appeared before me last night in my sleep a messenger of God, bright and with radiance about his head who spoke into my ear. He said, clearly and forcefully, 'The day has come. The hour has come. The time is nigh for you to begin your work about your Father's business. Do not linger any longer. Be at it.' He kicked another stone. Do you think, Chaim, that I am to begin my calling, even at age twelve that I am, of teaching and preaching?"

"Maybe so. It may be that you are to begin your serious studies with the elder priests." I breathed a deep breath. "Perhaps being in the Holy City as we are is a propitious omen. Perhaps you are to listen and learn, and maybe even to teach, while you are here this very day of your life. I think that is so," I said. "Yes, it is so."

Jesus remained silent for a while, deep in thought. Then he spoke again. "The messenger that spoke to me last night reminded me of my mission here on earth. He said that it would be easy for me to begin my earthly career. He said the time is nigh."

I could see that he was troubled at making this final—and most central—decision of his childhood. I could see that he was ready to accept the weight of the world that would very soon bear down upon his shoulders. He was a strong boy and I was confident that he would be wise in making his decision.

He decided well.

The Seder Feast

The seven days of Passover brought new experiences to Jesus.

A friend of Mary and Joseph's named Shalva, meaning, "Tranquility," who happened to live in Jerusalem, invited all of us to her home for the feast. "I am grateful to be among these friends at Passover," I said as I looked around the room and looked into each face. "I want to enjoy each Pesach that remains in my life. Blessings to all."

"Thank you, Chaim. You look good today. We are blessed to have you here."

Shalva busied herself with last-minute preparations. "Welcome to my home, dear friends of mine. Welcome Mary and Joseph. Welcome Jesus. Welcome Chaim," Shalva said. "*Chag Pesach Sameach* to each of us. Happy Passover!"

"Yes, *Chag Pesach Sameach*," wished Joseph to the table. "Happy Passover to us all."

"And *be'te-avon*," enjoined Shalva. "Good appetite to each of us."

Each of us found our appropriate place at the table. Each of us was hungry from the day's activities but remembered our proper manners in this celebration. We waited until our host invited us to partake.

Shalva continued. Her tone of voice was sober because this evening was the first ceremony of the Passover, and it set the tone for the rest of the meal. "I have been at work cleaning this home until it is spotlessly clean. Can you see? I know you can smell the fresh kitchen aromas. We are ready for the celebration to begin."

"I know you have been working diligently," said Mary, admiring the polished stoneware and the fine linens laid out on the table. "You are a gracious host."

"Yes, the first thing I did was to gather all *hamez* from the house and remove it. Our Scriptures in Exodus strictly forbid us from having any leavened or baked products made with any form of yeast. I removed all bread, cereal, and pasta that had been allowed to rise or swell with yeast."

"What did you do with it?" asked Jesus.

"I did several things. I burned some of it that was too old to be tasty. I ate some of the cereals with my breakfasts. Some of the pastas I gave to the hungry people living on the streets. The beer I poured out into the street where it dried in the air overnight. I followed the prescription of the law faithfully, and all of these things I did seven days ago. No trace of them remains."

"I am pleased with your preparations," said Joseph. "Exodus is important to us because it describes how Moses led our enslaved people out of Egypt. Exodus gives us the purpose of this Passover celebration."

Shalva continued. "We know that six foods are required to be on the Seder plate. Because Passover occurs in Nissan, in the spring, the foods on the plate symbolize, each in their own way, the reenactment of that escape. Karpas is a green vegetable—tonight we have parsley—that represents rebirth and rejuvenation in the springtime. We dip this food in saltwater and eat it. The saltwater represents the tears our ancestors shed during their years of enslavement.

"Maror is a bitter herb that reminds us of the embittered lives of the slaves held in Egypt. I grew this horseradish in my own garden. Mary, do you grow horseradish in your garden at home?"

"No, not this year, but I did grow some last season."

"I mixed some of the horseradish with charoset," Shalva continued. "See, this is the charoset." She touched the bowl with her fingers. "It is a pasty mixture of nuts, dates, apples, wine, and cinnamon. Its symbolism is that it reminds us of the mortar that our enslaved ancestors used to build the storehouses for the Pharaohs. *We* built their civilization. *We* made them powerful."

I could not wait to taste Shalva's charoset. Each year it seems to leave more and more aftertaste on my tongue, and I enjoy that. I should shame myself, for eating the Seder feast is not about taste, but about tradition and obeying the laws as handed down to us by the prophets.

Our host looked around the table at each of us. I think she was pleased at her preparations. "Zero'ah is a shank of lamb—really, only the bone and a little meat—that is infused with garlic, pepper, and other spices. It represents the sacrificed lamb that God directed us to slaughter and eat of its meat. With its blood, we then paint the lintels of each house as a symbol that death shall pass over us. It is written in Exodus." Jesus and I exchanged quick glances with each other, remembering the long conversations we had had over the years about this very subject. I know he will eat the full Seder meal because of its importance to our traditions.

Shalva continued. Beitza is a chicken's egg boiled hard. It reminds us of the newness of springtime; some people say it reminds them of fertility. It reminds us, too, that we Jews were reborn when we escaped from slavery.

"Matzot is a flat, dry bread made only of plain flour and water. It is a reminder of the tradition to abstain from any leavened foods during the seven days. We observe that and all traditions here."

Wine to me is not anything special because I drink wine daily with my meals. But at the Seder feast, wine is a special part of the ceremony. The adults at the table are required to drink four cups of wine over the course of the ceremony. Four cups of wine represent the four stages of the exodus: freedom, deliverance, redemption, and release. A goblet of wine is placed at the Seder table for Elijah the Prophet in the hope that he will join the celebration and partake of the wine. Because Jesus was not yet a man, he did not drink the wine. Shalva remembered to have a good supply of grape juice ready that Jesus could drink with the rest of us.

Prayers floated from all lips, blessing the gathering and thanking God for their many blessings.

Shalva even provided for us expensive spices of saffron, cinnamon, and ginger for flavorings; calamus for the scenting of the air; and a profusion of balm of Gilead to represent the love present within her home. At the conclusion of the celebration, Shalva provided us with myrtle berries to chew to sweeten our breaths. A musician named Liron, meaning, "My Song" or "My Joy," played melodies on his seven-stringed lyre.

After the joyous celebration, Jesus wondered, in secret with himself, if Passover could be celebrated without the requirement and spectacle of slaughtering animals. He wondered if that ceremonious week could be celebrated properly without that rite.

Ach! I almost forgot to explain that the meaning of the word Seder means, "Order," and the feast is undeniably an orderly ceremony. We celebrate it in fifteen steps. The steps must be obeyed and obeyed in the proper order, because the laws demand it be celebrated that way. And we did celebrate the feast according to the law.

The Consecration Rituals

The next day, Jesus underwent the consecration rituals with other boys that dedicated them as new citizens of Israel. It was at this ceremony that he and all boys assumed the yoke of the Law.

"*Mazal tov*, Yeshi. Congratulations on your attainment." Mary hugged her son softly.

After, he walked through the Temple with his mother and father, listening to his father explain the history and purpose of the corridors, courts, and galleries. Always, Jesus tried to connect Joseph's interpretations with those interpretations he had been formulating in his own mind in the past few years. This trip to the Temple was a lesson in Jewish history for the boy. All proper young men made the trip with their parents in order to prepare for the next year's induction into manhood. It was schooling for the soul.

This day, being anticlimactic compared to the ceremony, Joseph showed Jesus places within the Temple where Jesus could listen to lectures by the priests. To dismiss the frustration of not being a man, Jesus kept himself outside the balustrade that segregated all persons who were not full citizens of Israel. His youth kept self-control upon his curiosity, in that he restrained himself from asking the many questions that surged through his fertile mind. However, he did attend as many lectures as he could in the outer courts. He knew how important it was to be with ordinary citizens in ordinary settings, for that was a theme threading throughout his young life. Next year, at age thirteen when he became a man before God, he would participate fully with the men of Israel.

His time would come.

The Temple teemed with all manner of people during the Passover week. Joseph could not control what activity that went on; Jesus had to see with his own eyes the happenings within those walls. What disturbed Jesus most was the unruly crowds in the Court of the Gentiles within the Temple. Loud talking and profanity, shoving, and rude drinking all lent to a carnival atmosphere in God's house. Fishermen, lumbermen in their leathers, beggars in rags, and the lame—all were there. One blind man, squatting on a ragged mat and both eyes as dark as charcoal, looked left and right hopelessly. He lifted his begging cup, chanting, "Alms for the poor, alms for the poor." Women, too, added to the mix. Women carried babies at breast, some without a wet-cloth. Some brazen women drank as the men drank. Sunburned farmers and shepherds rounded out the crowd. Day laborers, shopkeepers, country priests, pilgrims, artisans, farmers, and merchants on mules all added turmoil to the throng. Animals on their noisy way to slaughter donated to the din.

The Court of the Priests held the altar dedicated to killing of droves of animals. Jesus, the nature-loving boy, sickened at that place in the Temple, even though he had not seen it with his own eyes. He knew that the Court of the Gentiles, however awful, was tame by comparison to what happened in the Court of the Priests.

Everyone in Jesus' circle of friends knew what he thought of the altar. Even though he despised what it stood for, he knew the deeper meaning of it. To Jesus, the altar was that place in consciousness where we were willing to give up the lower thought to the higher thought. It was the place where we traded the personal for the impersonal, the animal for the divine. He felt that any altar, whether used to burn incense or flesh, symbolized the establishment of permanent resolutions of covenants with the higher law of obedience.

CHAPTER 25

6 CE

∿∽∪⌣∿

Where Is Yeshi?

Preparing the morning meal was the first undertaking facing Mary as they prepared to depart from Jerusalem. Nothing could prevent her from following her prescribed routine. Breakfast was not a large meal.

I miss my home. I miss my own oven and my own cook fires, reminisced Mary. *If I were at home, I would serve warm breads, cheese, fruits, raisins, or anything else left over from the evening meal. On many mornings in my home, I might boil some barley in milk to prepare a thin porridge. I want my meals to be nutritious for my family.*

She sighed and looked around at the other women stooping over the cooking fires. *Like them, my work is never done. Each day I grind the grains and bake the breads, milk the goats and make the cheese, and prepare the fish or maybe chicken into suitable dishes for the evening meal. But because I love my family, my work is not drudgery; it is a gift I give to them.*

However, because today they would be traveling with the caravan, she would serve foods she had saved over the past few days. Luck was with her and the family, as she had accumulated enough food to prepare a thick pottage of lentils and beans and flavor it generously with peppers and hot spices. *This meal is a propitious beginning to the day's travel. Nothing will go wrong this day. Love is the way I walk in gratitude.*

Again Mary remembered. She remembered the good times, the prosperous times that had filtered into their lives back in Nazareth. *In those few precious seasons when God was extra good to us, I prepared dough of roasted barley, honey, and assorted nuts. I formed it with my hands into patties and baked them in my oven. Maybe I prepared boiled eggs or pickled eggs, and added to the meal fragrant fish sauce poured over freshly slain quails. Thank you, God, for my abundance.*

But that was ages ago; this was now.

In the distance, Mary could hear the sounds of morning. Shops opened and herders drove their animals to the slaughtering. She could smell the wood fires and the dung fires roasting fat left over from the sacrifices. She loved the activity but she loved her own home even more. *I miss my children, each one at home with Chava. I know she is taking good care of them for me. God bless her for her generosity.*

After breakfast, Mary busied herself with packing the baskets and the bundles with the items for the trip back to Nazareth. She found room for the tunic and mantle she wore for Jesus' consecration rituals, Joseph's extra mantle, and extra sandals for each they had purchased from the street sellers. After all, were they not entitled to buy a little something for themselves? Mary did buy a pretty embroidered linen that she intended to sew into a new veil for herself. Biscuits, some figs, and dates were included in her possessions. And certainly goat skins filled with fresh well water. She had no time to think of Jesus' whereabouts. She knew his temperament well enough to understand that he could be visiting with any number of neighbors who would be traveling in the caravan with them. And what about his playmates?—Of course he could be playing with any of them.

She was keenly aware that Jesus was on the verge of manhood. That was the point of the consecration rites. Why should she worry about his getting lost? For a boy of his intelligence, that would be impossible.

Leaving Jerusalem was not easy for either Joseph or Mary. I know. I know how hard it was to leave that precious city, that jewel of the desert. I have had to depart from its gates many times over the years. Each year on the return trip, my eyes would glisten with tears as I thought of the joy the Temple radiated to me. To be even in the same city as the Temple was a true blessing. We of Jewish background are in favor with God to know of its beauty and meaning.

The trip home was not an arduous one. The crowdedness of the caravan made the miles seem almost easy. Jesus of course was somewhere in the moving multitude; by all logic, he just had to be. Near the end of the day's travel, Mary began to ask if anyone had seen her Yeshi. Nobody had.

"Joseph, where is Yeshi?"

"He is here. Of course he is here—somewhere. Where else could he be?"

"Chaim," she asked of me, "have you seen any sign of my son?"

I could only answer honestly. "No, I have not seen him for many hours."

Alarm became real. "Do not unpack the tent. We must go back. We must go back to find him. It is what we must do." Just to be sure of herself, Mary ran frantically among the families who were beginning the evening's routine to ask if anyone had seen her boy. Her quest was futile.

"We will travel by the moonlight. It is our only option. We leave now." Mary's face told Joseph all he needed to know. He had come to learn her facial expressions over the past twelve years, and this was not one of the more pleasant looks.

Joseph knew how special the annual pilgrimage to Jerusalem was to me. For that reason, my young friend kept an open eye on me, to look after me in his own fatherly way. "Chaim, will you come with us—Mary and me—when we go back. We need to find our boy. We need to know where he is. Maybe you, in your wisdom, can help us to know where he might be. We are hoping he is still within the safety of the walls."

I was humbled that Joseph would ask me to accompany them. He knew of my age and my condition. I did not take any time to think of an answer. "Of course I will go with you." I merely thought that he did not want to leave me alone. Ach! He knew how many friends I have! I would have been just fine in the caravan. I would not have been lonely. Now it was my turn to be a father to Joseph. How could I abandon the lovely pair in their desperation?

Disappointment

We lost no time in turning around. We hailed our fellow travelers as we hurried in the opposite direction, wishing them good travel. It was near dark as we set aside our fatigue and plunged into our mission. Joseph saw to it that Mary was the one to ride the donkey. The donkey carried their unemployed tent and the rest of their belongings on his back, as he had done all day. I shouldered my meager belongings and fell silent as we walked. I could not help myself but to lag behind the donkey, faithful creature that he was. My spirit was strong, stronger than anything I knew except God. But my legs were not what they were. Hours later, we paused to take refreshment. Mary insisted that I be the one to ride the donkey. I did until late in the night, when the stars rolled to the other side of the sky. Only near dawn did we stop to rest ourselves and the beast. That was most necessary and welcome.

The rest is indeed welcome. We have come a long way in our search for the boy. We are fatigued. We are dusty and have thirst. I trust that Jesus is in good hands of loving care, wherever he is. Carrying Chaim is an honor. The man radiates love. He is a blessing. But I am concerned of his health. He is not strong anymore, as a young man. Let me not forget my function.

The city was not as I remembered it. The excitement was missing; the hubbub was gone. Now Jerusalem was just another city recovering from just another Passover celebration. As if Passover was ordinary.

Everywhere we looked. Jesus was nowhere. The first place we entered was the Court of the Gentiles, inside the Temple, praying as we searched. But the Court of the Gentiles covers thirty-five acres, more than three times the size of the village of Nazareth! Our hours of searching there only exhausted us, to the point of forgetting to inquire of any soldier of authority if he had seen a lost boy.

Once outside the Temple, we looked in narrow doorways that led into small courtyards. We asked in alleyways. We searched the open spaces. It was always the same response—frowns, questioned looks, indifference. How could we have missed him? Mary tried to describe him, but the people were too busy cleaning up after the pilgrims who had swept through their home to give us a considered answer. "His eyes shine, his clump of hair is the color of mustard seed, he has freckles that are the color of toasted barley." But it was to no advantage. Even in the cardo did we search, where the bakeries and butcheries thrived, where the smelly tanners and the muscular smiths and all manner of workmen were cleaning up their places of work. All issued the same result. This great work we did in vain for two full days. Fatigue should have been a factor, but none of us three showed any ill effects of walking and looking so continuously.

Mary: *Why did I ever abandon my son? What was I thinking? I was careless to think he was capable of bringing himself to the caravan so he could come home with us.*

Oh, Yeshi, if you are out there somewhere, show your face to me. I am your mother! I gave you life! You sprang from my womb. Do you know how much that pained me? Now I feel a different kind of pain for you, a different kind of love for you. You are a mature boy now, my Yeshi. Come into my arms so that I might cry tears into your hair and wrap my arms around your precious head. Cannot you see how I suffer without you!

Dearest God on high, hear my anguish. Let me see my boy's face, his rumpled hair, and the boyish look on his face before he is too soon a man. Oh! His radiant face. I am in your grace. I am in your love. I am yours.

6 CE

Relief

On the third day of scouring Jerusalem, in the afternoon, we sat to rest at a public table. I knew Joseph; I knew his character. When he wrinkled his forehead and scratched his beard in his thoughtful manner that he has, I knew he was inspired greatly. "I am going to the praetorium. The soldiers there will know what to do. Mary, you and Chaim wait here. I pray that Jesus is safe. May God be with us." I was astounded that the quiet talking carpenter would be of such demeanor as to even consider such a move. All Jews know the intimidation that surrounds the headquarters of the Roman army, and it is great.

Joseph's admonition to remain at rest did not prefigure well with Mary. "My baby is missing for three days. I cannot sit at this table and be idle. He may be sick. He may be hurt. I must be with Joseph to help find my boy. Chaim, come with me."

The next event I remember was that she and I were on the heels of Joseph, scanning both sides of the landscape for the absent Jesus as we went our way to find him. Again there were three pairs of eyes, looking and listening for any sign of authority.

I knew that on this third day of searching for Jesus, we would find him whole and safe; we would find new meaning in our lives by finding him. Somehow, this idea awakened me to become more alive and more awake to the mundane events flooding us every day. I could not rid from my mind the concept of the third day—the third day—as being as powerful as it was. I did not know its implication, to be sure, but I knew that the concept stayed mightily in my mind.

I had seen the praetorium many times over the years, but only from the outside. In its core, it was a barracks for the soldiers, but in its reality, it was a fortress because of its integration into the walls of Jerusalem. The king living here today was Antipas—governor, really—son of Herod the Great who built this magnificent Temple. Have ten years past since Herod the Great died? Ordinary Roman generals must live in a tent in the desert but because this is Jerusalem, the soldiers bivouacked here enjoyed this opulence. Inside the gate of the praetorium lie groomed gardens and sparkling pools of clear water that served no practical purpose to common men like us other than to play a feast on our eyes. The inward parts had the largeness and form of a palace. On the floor of one room, Joseph found a mosaic so brilliantly colored that burning lamps set it afire. The windows offered sunlit scenes so colorful that Joseph could not remove his eyes from them. The walls were stuccoed to resemble bossed ashlars. From the ceiling, fully twelve feet high, hung candelabra of countless branches fitted with scented and smokeless candles of beeswax. Courts and places for bathing and recreating were everywhere. At this time of year, all the gardens were lush and verdant.

We found silence in nearly every deserted bend, save for the faint echoes of our feet upon the floor. The towered corners of the building reached to the sky. Their purpose was to serve as observation posts for scrutinizing our people, especially during feasts, that we might not make any disturbances. Arches covered the streets that connected it to the nearby Temple. We soon learned that when the pilgrims returned to their homes, so too did Antipas and his retinue retire to their country estates.

Out of nowhere appeared a young centurion, striding rigidly and on patrol of the near-quiet praetorium. Other than the scar across his cheek, he appeared too inexperienced to hold such power. The helmet atop his head shone in the sunlight, and its burgundy and white plumes on top made him seem too tall and too ostentatious. Symbolic shields across his breastplate signified his rank. A sheathed sword hung on his belt. Shiny shin guards met his black boots. A guardsman flanked each side of him, adding further to his ominous image.

In her broken Latin and through her tears, Mary asked—beseeched—him for his help to find Jesus. I could understand most of what they said, as could Joseph. Without a word, the centurion turned and pointed a finger across the square, leading our eyes down an avenue of shiny floor tiles.

The direction was toward the Temple.

Mary's eyes shone like suns. Remembering her manners, she knelt briefly at the boots of the centurion in gratitude, then lifted her skirts to her knees and ran free-legged. I smiled. What else could I do? And then, as if she and I communicated with our minds, she stopped and returned to me. My mind was grateful. *Mary, oh Mary! You are thoughtful! You did not have to turn around. You did not have to walk by my side and urge me on by my arm.* Ach! I could only walk as fast as my legs would carry me. Joseph was proud of his jewel Mary, I knew, to be caring for old Chaim. We made our way across the plazas and down the avenue toward the Temple.

Finally, inside the Temple, behind the portico, and beyond the last line of columns, we arrived at the Temple's vast library where we spied Jesus.

There he was! He was clean and healthy, undisturbed at having been the focus of such a severe search. To be sure, he did not even know he was missing.

Mary sprinted. She could not have clattered any faster over the marble tiles if she tried. Joseph was close on her heels. I, I managed as best I could to reach the commotion. My eyes and ears failed me not, for they told me more than enough. It appeared to me that the boy *ignored* his mother! *Completely!*

It was not as if Jesus were in that library alone. Scribes sat with bent heads at tables overflowing with parchments, papyrus, and scratching quills, copying symbols from one document to another. In the air were smells of burning oil, inkpots, and wine.

Encircling Jesus, seated on tapestried cushions, were four wise-aged men. Indeed, they were the Pharisees—those teachers, sages, and ever the sagacious men of the community. They were the most learned in all of Judea. Certainly, the duty of the Pharisees was to observe the rites and ceremonies of the Jewish law, and to ensure all formality was enforced strictly and without even the smallest of deviations. To Mary, the men did not exist. Only Jesus was there. The men at the tables paused their labor and stood upon the arrival of us strangers.

"Yeshua, where have you been? Where are your manners? For three days, your father and I have been searching for you. My heart is drained of strength for you. Do you hear me? Do you understand what I say? Look at me. Look at me! Say something."

Nothing.

"Look at me! Say something, young man! We sought you in every street and alley and courtyard in Jerusalem. We looked in the hills and in the orchards and inns. We feared you were hurt, my son. We were devastated at your absence. Even Chaim helped us to look for you."

She paused to catch her breath. Then calmly and quietly, like a whisper, she said, "Yeshi, please, look at me and say something." She remembered the scrap of cloth that held the secret lock of Jesus' hair in her innermost pocket; touching it with her fingertips gave her a sense of relief.

He turned to look at her, ever so obliquely, with a hint of annoyance.

It was only then that Mary noticed the small swarm of men surrounding her boy. Now about her wits, she silenced herself, rose to her full height, and looked in turn at each man firmly. "Gentlemen, this is my son. He has been lost for three days. His father and I have been searching frantically for him. We are exhausted. We are frustrated. We want nothing more than to take him home where we belong. We are family. We feared for his safety—nay, for his life."

Here she breathed deeply.

"And I finally find him here, in this dark and distant corner of the Temple, with you, strangers all. I do not know what you have been telling him. I do not know what he has told you. And forthrightly, that is not important. What is important is the fact that you held him here against his will, against his resolve. He has been hostage in and to your circle of chatter. What am I to think of you and your assembly?"

It was only at this time that Joseph could speak. "Mary, please. The boy is unharmed. The boy is safe. Look at him. *Look* at him. He is our son. We have reason to celebrate, not to shout angry cries to the air. We need not be upset. The universe has answered our prayers. And he is here, before our eyes—look, do you see?—unharmed and perfect in every way."

I was in awe at the great weight that lifted from Mary's shoulders. I had not ever seen her so fraught with emotion. I could tell that she felt relieved, unburdened at finding Jesus. If only she would—

"Woman!" Jesus now. "Woman, why do you wail so grievously? Why do you let your heart cry out so thunderously? These men are my friends. These men are my teachers. And I, theirs. I have not been lost. I have not gone astray like a sheep in the night. It was my decision to stay here after the Pesach, to grow and to learn with these teachers. Mother, be at peace. Do you not know that I am to be here, in this House of God, with the Father's Spirit that dwells within each of us? This is my place to be in this now time and place. I am at peace, for I am with God, as are you."

One of the teachers spoke. He was the one Jesus had been so deeply absorbed with in conversation when Mary and Joseph and I first saw the young man. "Go, son, go with your mother and father. Return to your home. Go to where you must be. We learned together and taught together, we did, and each of us is richer for it." He turned to speak to Mary. "You do not understand what has transpired between us. Only he"—suggesting Jesus—"understands. This boy is an architect of thought. He is brilliant for his age. Perhaps he is of no age, as we humans know it. Release your concerns to the God above. Hold this day in your heart. He is ready to go home, to be with his family. Journey in peace."

Enthusiasm. The afternoon's sun shone the entire Temple in an orange glow that I had not seen before. At the center of its glow stood Jesus, afire in his determination to know all he could know and to be the great illuminator of Light that he was to be. I knew he was living and loving completely because, as he exemplified that afternoon, he was full of enthusiasm and joy for the task he was to undertake.

Reflections

Ach! What am I supposed to say? It was all such a blur before my eyes. The way we hurried back to Jerusalem to find Jesus. The way we searched endlessly and fruitlessly. The way the boy affronted his mother. Is that the manner of the youth these days? Jesus is a smart boy, to be sure. It is my observation that his maturity led him to seek out those teachers, to learn all he could from them. His time has arrived to depart from his boyhood and seek the experiences of a man. It is how he will grow. It is the only way there is for him.

The fact that he disrespected his mother with his exasperating behavior is not for me to judge. Only God can judge because only God can create. Because we are all of God, that makes all of us one flesh and one mind. The behavior of one is the behavior of all. Even the trees and the animals and fishes and the rocks are of God. Everything is connected. All are one. How can the left hand disregard the right one?

That evening in the tents was a quiet one. Each of us was lost in our own memories of the day. It was a landmark for each of us, especially for Jesus. Even though his head was swirling with unasked questions and insufficient answers, he was at great peace. I do not think he slept at all.

I echo Chaim's thoughts about the lessons learned today. You are a man trapped in a boy's body. You are well on your way to fulfilling the role of the Messiah. Glory be to you.

Jesus: Ilan, I hear your cries, I feel your anguish over me. Fear not. Rest this evening. I am content to be wherever God sends me. These past days I was directed to be in the Temple with those learned men as my teachers.

You do know that your mother cried for your safety? And your father, too, was crying on the inside for your wellbeing.

Jesus: Yes, that I know. But as you know, it was my duty to be in my Father's house.

I accept that.

The next day's heat roused us early from our pallets. Mary, bless her goodness, noticed my increasing limp. To me, it was nothing beyond normal. Mary thought differently. "Chaim, my dear friend, you struggle to keep up with the donkey. Come, you sit. You ride and rest your bones. I want you to do so. Please allow me to walk at your side."

"Yes, do," insisted Joseph. "Mary knows best."

How could I break their hearts? For that day's ride, I rode the donkey and the three of them walked beside me. I admit that taking the burden off my legs felt good. Too, my chest felt sore on the inside. I think the donkey knew my condition. I think the donkey stepped gingerly over the rock and scree to make my ride ever more comfortable. How precious is the ride of life? There is always a new notion to learn, and my lesson for that day was to learn to accept graciousness when it was offered. That night, I slumbered as I remembered the baby Jesus sleeping in the manger so many years ago. How sweet my dream!

CHAPTER 27

6 CE

∿‿⌣‿ᴧ

Chaim's Victory

"Wake up, old man! Wake up! The sun shines this splendid today. God's bounty is at hand." Joseph busied himself by helping Mary to prepare for the day's walk. "Wake up, Chaim, as I furl the tent into the donkey's pannier. We will be on the road soon."

As he said these words, Joseph could not help but notice that the morning air seemed crisper, somehow more enlivening than it should have been. *Is something happening that I am not aware of?* conjectured Joseph. "Does anyone notice the feeling in the air?" he asked no one directly, not to Jesus, not to Mary. "What is it that is different about this morning?"

"Husband of mine, what do you say?" asked Mary, looking up at Joseph as she stirred the morning lentil soup. "What do you feel?"

"I feel good today. The air feels especially fresh today, I think. Today is a good day." He turned to look again at Chaim's tent. A frown crossed his brow. "He is not awake."

"What is it, father? Does Chaim not wake?" Jesus asked, yawning and stretching as he crawled from his tent. "He is an early riser. I know he likes to wake early and see the new sun arise."

"You are correct, my son. Chaim does not sleep late. I hope he is well. We all had a very hard walk yesterday."

"I do hope he feels well this day," offered Mary. "I remember that he complained about his chest aching yesterday. That is why he rode the donkey. He will be up soon; do not be anxious."

"I will look in his tent," volunteered Joseph.

"Son, please help me with—" Mary began.

"—No, no, it cannot be. It cannot be!" interrupted Joseph. "IT CANNOT BE!"

"What is it?" cried Mary. "Joseph, what is it?" She dropped the spoon, lifted the front of her skirts, and ran to where Joseph stood at Chaim's tent. "Tell me!"

Joseph looked at her softly and rested his hands on her shoulders. "He is quite still and peaceful. He has left this world. He is departed in his sleep." Joseph felt the tear forming on his cheek. "He is at peace with his God above."

"He is gone?"

"Yes, Chaim has left his body."

"Blessings upon his soul," wept Mary into Joseph's chest. "He is a good man."

"He is gone to his Father above," added Jesus quietly. "He is my friend and I love him. Now he lives in the arms of the Father. Shalom to you, my friend, shalom to you."

What a privilege it was to carry Chaim on my back for his last day. I am honor-struck. He was not anybody's burden, ever. Rather, he was a light and a delight to love. He was love and wisdom in its truest manifestation. Jesus, if you can witness me today, this hour, hear my words. Be like Chaim. Be love. Be strength. Be life. Above all, be the Messiah you are meant to be.

BIBLIOGRAPHY

Bishop, Jim. *The Day Christ Was Born, The Day Christ Died* (New York: Galahad Books, 1993)

Butler, Sandra, Reverend. Numerous talks and classes given at Unity of Fairfax, Fairfax, Virginia, that rendered metaphysical symbolism

Cahill, Thomas. *The Gifts of the Jews: How a Tribe of Desert Nomads Changed the Way Everyone Thinks and Feels* (New York: Doubleday, 1998)

Charlesworth, James H. *Jesus and the Dead Sea Scrolls* (New York: Doubleday, 1992)

Dobson, Danae and Dobson, Dr. James. *Parables for Kids* (Wheaton, Illinois: Tyndale House Publishers, Inc., 2005)

Brown, Raymond E. *An Introduction to the New Testament* (New York: Doubleday, 1997)

Cannon, Dolores. *Jesus and the Essenes: Fresh insights into Christ's Ministry and the Dead Sea Scrolls* (The Hollies, Wellow, Bath, UK: Gateway Books, 1992)

Easley, Kendell, H. *The Illustrated Guide to Biblical History* (Nashville, Tennessee: Holman Bible Publishers, 2003)

Embry, Margaret. *Everyday Life in Bible Times* (Nashville, Tennessee: Lion Publishing, 1994)

Fillmore, Charles. *Keep a True Lent* (Unity Village, MO: Unity Books, 1959)

Fillmore, Charles. *Metaphysical Bible Dictionary* (Unity Village, MO: Unity Books, 1931)

Fillmore, Charles. *The Revealing Word* (Lee's Summit, MO: Unity School of Christianity, 1959)

Fillmore, Charles. *The Twelve Powers of Man* (Lee's Summit, MO: Unity School of Christianity, 1930)

Girzone, Joseph F. *Jesus: His Life and Teachings* (New York: Doubleday, 2000)

Gundry, Robert H. *A Survey of the New Testament,* third edition (Grand Rapids, Michigan: Zondervan Publishing House, 1994)

Johnson, Donna, Reverend. Numerous talks and classes given at Unity of Fairfax, Fairfax, Virginia, that rendered metaphysical symbolism

MacGregor, Jerry and Pyrs, Marie. *1001 Surprising Things You Should Know about the Bible* (Grand Rapids, Michigan: Baker Books, 2002)

McDowell, Josh. *More Than a Carpenter* (Wheaton, Illinois: Tyndale House Publishers, Inc., 1977)

Miller, Calvin, ed. *The Book of Jesus* (New York: Simon & Schuster, 1996)

Oke, Janette. *I Wonder . . . Did Jesus Have a Pet Lamb?* (Bloomington, Minnesota: Bethany House Publishers, 2004)

Osborne, Mary Pope. *The Life of Jesus in Masterpieces of Art* (New York: Penguin Group, 1998)

Owens, Clifford P., compiler. *A Story of Jesus* (Virginia Beach, Virginia: A.R.E. Press, 1963)

Peters, F. E., Professor. *Judaism. Christianity, and Islam: The Monotheists,* Recorded Lectures (New York University: Recorded Books, LLC, 2003)

Petersham, Maud and Miska. *The Christ Child: A reverent picture book of the greatest and best-loved story in the world* (Garden City, New York: Doubleday, 1931)

Rice, Anne. *Christ the Lord* (New York: Random House, 2005)

Richardson, Joy, ed. *Jesus of Nazareth: A Life of Christ through Pictures* (New York: Simon & Schuster, 1994)

Rosen, Moishe. *Y'shua* (Chicago, Illinois: The Moody Bible Institute of Chicago, 1982)

Schucman, Helen and Thetford, William T., eds. *A Course in Miracles, Original Edition* (Omaha, Nebraska: Course in Miracles Society, Public Domain Document)

Smith, Patricia T. and Soderlind, Kirsten. *The Miracle of the Loaves and Fishes* (Alexandria, Virginia: Time Life, 1996)

Urantia Foundation. *The Urantia Book* (Chicago, Illinois: Urantia Foundation, 1955)

Van Biema, David. "Jerusalem at the Time of Jesus," *Time Magazine*, p. 46, April 16, 2001

Wangerin, Walter Jr. *Jesus: A Novel* (Grand Rapids, Michigan: Zondervan, 2005)

Warch, William A. *How to Use Your Twelve Gifts from God* (Anaheim, California: Christian Living Publishing Company, 1976)

Many web sites